When Corporal Brian Haas took in a fellow marine's comatose younger brother in an attempt to figure out how to heal him, he never could have imagined the chain of events that it would set off. The testing his patient — Bailey Dyer — had been forcibly subjected to changed his DNA. Bailey had ended up turning into a paranormal creature called a shifter, giving him the ability to turn into a sentient cheetah at will.

Upon learning of shifters' existence, Brian agrees to relocate to the mountains of Colorado to help his buddy and the shifters looking into those targeting them. He builds a new bunker, preparing for when the thugs of the shadow military branch come calling. Brian knows it's just a matter of time, and he has every intention of making sure he and his new friends will be ready for them.

Brian spots a cheetah trotting into his yard. Assuming it's Bailey, he doesn't think anything about it . . . until it starts purring and rubbing up against him. This cheetah is not his ex-patient. When the man shifts, Brian finds himself face-to-face with a blond calling himself David Preston, and he seems to be just as confused by his sudden infatuation as Brian . . . until David calls Brian his mate.

Brian realizes his life is about to be turned upside-down all over again . . . if the confused altered can come to grips with his own changes.

The Altered's Atonement
Copyright © 2022 Charlie Richards
ISBN: 978-1-4874-3604-9
Cover art by Angela Waters

Published by eXtasy Books Inc

Look for us online at:
www.eXtasybooks.com

THE ALTERED'S ATONEMENT
WOLVES OF STONE RIDGE: BOOK FIFTY-EIGHT

BY

CHARLIE RICHARDS

CHAPTER ONE

Corporal Brian Haas rhythmically swung the axe, splitting log after log. Humming under his breath, he relished the burn in his muscles. The simple act worked just about every part of his body, from his neck to his calves. Considering he used firewood to help maintain his off-the-grid lifestyle, he did it nearly every day to keep his wood stores up.

Pausing, Brian set aside the axe and stretched his arms over his head. He twisted left and right a few times. Feeling the pop in his back, he grunted softly with pleasure.

The pops and cracks reminded Brian that he wasn't as young as he used to be. For the most part, he didn't feel old, but there were times when his body reminded him that he was forty-eight years old, and he'd been discharged from the military due to injury.

On a mission, Brian's *Humvee* had hit an IED. His team had been fortunate, as they'd all walked away with their lives. Brian had sustained lacerations in his left thigh from flying debris. While he'd healed, his leg would never have the strength it had once had, and he'd been forced to retire before he'd planned.

As it had turned out, Brian found it a good thing. He'd grown tired of the bullshit bureaucracy that seemed to be taking over the military, not to mention the less-than-stellarly-researched assignments. That included the last one where he'd had chunks of his thigh muscle torn out of him by debris.

Yeah, Brian knew he'd become more than a little jaded. His whole damn team had been. Unfortunately, like him, most of them had at least a year and a half left to their service contract.

Then the IED.

While the rehabilitation had sucked, Brian knew it was the best thing that could have happened to him. He just felt bad that his buddy Ronan hadn't agreed. Still, looking back, Brian figured if Ronan had still been in the service, he wouldn't have been able to help his brother, Bailey.

With the turn of his thoughts, Brian snorted while rolling his eyes. "Bailey," he muttered under his breath before using a flannel shirt sleeve to wipe his brow. "God damned military experiments." Stacking a number of pieces of wood in his left arm before grasping another with his right, Brian began trudging toward the shelter where he stored his firewood. "Shifters and paranormals are real."

Brian still had a hard time believing the rabbit hole he'd fallen down. Except, as the saying went, seeing was believing. He'd seen shifters in action.

Hell, Brian had even met a vampire.

Back and forth, back and forth, Brian stored away his chopped wood while allowing his thoughts to ruminate over the events of the last, well, over a year.

After leaving the service, Brian had kept in touch with his closest comrades — Ronan Dyer being the top one — although there were a few others. He'd been his team's medic while in the service. Instead of pursuing that line of work, Brian had dropped out of society. He'd bought a hundred acres of secluded forestland with an old ramshackle cabin on it. After making the home just this side of livable, Brian had built a bunker and stocked supplies, using the cabin as a decoy.

After everything Brian had seen in the military, he knew the world was getting ready to implode — one way or another — and he planned to be ready for it.

Imagine Brian's surprise when, several years into his prepping, Ronan had contacted him about his brother. His buddy had busted his younger brother out of a military-funded lab, which had been disguised as a hospital. Ronan hadn't known how Bailey had ended up there, and his brother had been in a coma, so he hadn't been able to tell him.

All Ronan knew was that the military was after him, wanting Bailey back badly. They'd spread lies, tarnishing Ronan's record. Due to Brian's medical experience and his prepper lifestyle, Ronan had asked him to keep Bailey safe while he tried to figure out what was going on.

Brian had kept Bailey safe for nearly a year—even when a couple of military stooges had arrived and questioned him about Ronan and if he knew his whereabouts. Playing the eccentric prepper mountain man, he'd easily been able to send them on their way. Then he'd passed the names on to a hacker buddy of his, but the man hadn't been able to discover anything.

Ronan hadn't been able to do much either, considering he could barely stay in one place for long.

Everything had changed when Ronan had set up camp in the wrong forest. He'd been discovered by a wolf shifter who ended up being what they call mates. Evidently, that was a shifter's term for the other half of their soul.

Go figure. What are the odds?

Those wolf shifters had already dealt with people like the assholes who'd experimented on Bailey, and they were happy to help Ronan and Bailey. Their arrival had dragged Brian down the rabbit hole, too. He wasn't too proud to admit that discovering proof there were others on the earth had overloaded him, and he'd fainted.

Proof of a theory could do that to a man.

Chuckling under his breath, Brian put away the last pieces of wood. He'd burned through a lot more than he'd thought he would need over a Colorado winter, and he knew he would need to step it up over the summer to replenish his supplies. His prior home had been in the wilds of the Ozarks in Missouri, and while they did get snow, it didn't compare to the Colorado Rockies.

I'll get used to it.

Upon the revelation of shifters, Brian had been happy to throw his lot in with the guys. He recognized them as good folk. Brian had boarded up his place, locking down the facility, and had moved to pack land, where the wolves had set him up with a secluded place.

Hell, it was only accessible by four-wheel drive in the summer and snow machine in the winter.

Brian loved the seclusion.

Also, Brian could create any kind of shelter he wanted for the wolf pack. If someone came looking, he would have a place ready for them to fall back to that was easily defendable. Brian was building an underground tunnel system, a series of trap doors, and even ladders inside dead trees—which he'd reinforced with steel girders—that led to sniper nests hidden in the canopy.

To top it all off, Brian didn't have to pay for anything. Alpha Declan McIntire, the leader of the wolf shifter pack, had liked the idea of having a safe place to send those in his pack. While Declan shared his psyche with a wolf, he understood that not everyone was able to fight.

Those people needed a safe place to hide—should a real battle with the military ensue—and Brian was creating it.

While Brian knew Alpha Declan had faith that their CIA friends would take care of the problem from within, he'd seen far too much depravity in the world to believe that would work. The leaders of those experimenting on shifters were like the mythical hydra. If one head was cut off, two more would grow to take its place.

Sometimes, reality sucks.

Brian would be ready for it anyway.

Stopping on his small porch, Brian picked up a bottle of electrolyte water and chugged half the contents. He leaned a hip against the railing and mentally cataloged the next tasks on his list. As he did that, he lowered a hand and rubbed at his left thigh, massaging the scarred flesh beneath his cargo pants.

First, finish installing the security cameras at the north end.

That had been the last quadrant to be kitted out with the extensive surveillance he wanted in place. It had taken months, and a little help from a few of the more tech-savvy human mates of the pack, but he knew they were almost ready. After that, he would contact one of those same mates — a guy named Raul — to encrypt everything to his computer setup in the underground bunker.

Raul would be one of the humans who would bring his family there in the event that the worst should happen. A computer wiz, the man would help keep track of everything. At the same time, Raul would be protecting his adopted daughter, Lily. She was the niece of Raul's wolf shifter mate, Sean. Evidently, Lily's mother had passed in childbirth.

As Brian turned to head into the cabin, his stomach grumbled. "Right." He glanced over his shoulder at the sun blazing high in the sky. "First, a meal."

When Brian got into the swing of splitting firewood — *no pun intended, ha ha* — he knew he often lost track of time.

Brian left the front door open to encourage a breeze to flow through the house. To that end, he opened the window over the kitchen sink, too. Feeling the cool air flow over his sweat-drenched frame caused goose bumps to rise on his skin, hidden beneath his damp flannel shirt.

"Very nice."

Smiling, Brian quickly shucked the flannel shirt, followed by his undershirt. He draped them over the back of one of the small round dining room table's straight-backed chairs. Then he turned on the hot water tap before leaning against the counter and grabbing a hand towel.

After checking the heat of the water — and waiting another

thirty seconds for it to get hot—Brian lightly wet the towel. He rubbed it over his torso, cleaning his arms, chest, and pits. Finally, he grabbed his shirts again and took everything to the small laundry room off the kitchen, dumping them in the laundry basket.

Brian had set up an off-the-grid solar charging station to power not only the electronics, but also a few other basic necessities as well. When the time came, it would even heat the underground tunnels.

Right then, however, with it just being him around, Brian was happy to use the fireplace in the one-room cabin. The place didn't even have a bedroom. Even the bathroom was closed off by a curtain, although Brian never used it.

It wasn't as if there was anyone out there to see him wash, after all.

Still shirtless, Brian stepped through the back door. He crossed to his small propane grill and turned it on. While it heated, he returned to the kitchen to decide what to enjoy for his late lunch, his grumbling stomach encouraging him to choose quickly. Spotting what he wanted, he grabbed a bowl and plate from the cupboard and set them on his small prep counter.

Brian pulled out a pound of ground venison and unwrapped it before placing it in the bowl. Then he grabbed his small carton of eggs, cracked one into the bowl, and returned the carton to the fridge. Using his hip, Brian closed the door before sinking his hands into the bowl and massaging the raw egg into the meat. Once he had it mixed to his satisfaction, he formed three patties and placed them on the plate.

Using his elbow, Brian turned the hot water back on so he could wash his hands. He placed the bowl in the sink and filled it, planning to wash it later. Brian dried his hands, grabbed his salt and pepper shakers from the table, then picked up his burger plate.

Humming with anticipation, Brian headed back outside. He placed the patties on the heated grill, closed the cover, and returned inside. After placing the plate in the sink, he began pulling out the veggies he wanted on his burger — tomato, onions, and pickles. Brian carefully tore several large lettuce leaves off the head, intending to use them in lieu of a bun. Once he'd left the military, he didn't work out quite as much, so he did away with as many carbs as he could.

While prepping everything, Brian paused a couple of times to check his burgers, adding salt and pepper as needed, not to mention slices of goat cheese he carved off of a block he'd made himself. With everything ready and waiting on the small table, he headed to the grill once more. Just as he was setting the beautifully grilled patties on a clean plate, movement to his left caught his attention.

Brian's brows shot up as he watched a feline form round the corner of the cabin — a cheetah. He would have been concerned if he hadn't been privy to a few key pieces of information.

The experiments Bailey had been put through had been to insert shifter DNA into him. That had ended up giving him the ability to shift into that animal. Also, while in that form, Bailey was completely cognizant.

While Bailey didn't pop in on Brian often, the altered human would occasionally find his way out there when he needed a bit of solitude.

"Hey, Bailey," Brian greeted, grinning as the slender cheetah prowled toward him. "Did you smell the burgers and decide to stop by?"

Brian knew a shifter's sense of smell was even better than their animal's natural counterpart. He could only guess how far away the man could notice the scent of grilling meat.

"Let me take these inside," Brian continued as he turned off his grill and started toward the door. "I'll put these on the table and grab you some sweatpants while you shift."

To Brian's surprise, he didn't make it to the door. The cat bounded up to him, intercepting him. The tall feline's head reached Brian's belly, and he began rubbing his furred face against his abdominals.

Freezing, Brian stared at the shifter in shock, confusion filling him. He stared down at the cheetah, who, for all intents and purposes, seemed to be marking him. He opened his mouth to question Bailey, then snapped it shut just as quickly.

"Y-You're not Bailey," Brian whispered, seeing the subtle differences in the spot patterns than what was on Bailey's cat's fur. "Who are you?"

Brian knew he had to be a shifter, just from his actions. That meant he had to be one of Bailey's four team members. He'd never met any of them, but he knew all of them had been experimented on, too. Brian had also been told that their memories had been wiped, and a vampire had been brought in to help them.

So who is this?

"Come on, buddy," Brian urged, easing forward a step. "Let's go inside and eat." He carefully maneuvered sideways, although the cat didn't let him get far, following closely behind him. "We'll talk."

And figure out what the fuck is going on.

CHAPTER TWO

Unable to help himself, David Preston followed the stranger into the cabin. He kept his head close, needing more of the human's smell. His cat practically purred with the pleasurable way it lit up his senses.

David had never smelled anything so amazing as this guy.

The man set the plate containing the burger patties on a small round table standing in the left corner of the small cabin. Training made him sweep his gaze around the space, taking in the lay of the land—so to speak. There was a kitchen to the left, followed by a laundry and storage area. The rest of the floor sported a sleeper-sofa and a fireplace with a reclining chair before it. A book rested on a small table next to that.

There was a curtain in the far corner that could be used to close off the toilet and bathing area.

"So, you gonna shift, buddy?" the man asked, eyeing him warily. "You're one of Bailey's men, right?"

David hesitated, glancing toward the door. Except, even as he thought about running, his cat vehemently rejected the idea. While running through the forest as his cheetah, David's cat had noticed the unexpected scent and had run flat out toward it. Now, the beast refused to take one step toward the doorway.

Before David could figure out what to do, Bailey, in cheetah form, came barreling through the open front door. He skidded to a stop, sliding a few feet across the floor on his paws. Bailey's amber-eyed gaze peered around the room, seeming to take everything in at a glance.

A second later, Bailey began to shift. His former commanding officer, and now the person who David's cat thought of as their alpha, changed forms swiftly. Within half a minute, a naked Bailey rose to his feet.

Unable to help himself, David curled his lip and snarled in warning.

Bailey narrowed his eyes just a smidge before striding to the table. Grabbing the back of a chair, he pulled it close and used it to shield his nudity. His lips pulled into a tight scowl as he focused on David.

"What part of running together did you miss, David?" Bailey snapped, a growl in his voice. "Why the hell would you go tearing off like that?" Then he glanced toward the bearded man who David loved the smell of and stated, "Sorry about this, Brian." Then he refocused his scowl on David.

"No worries, Bailey. Figured he was one of yours," the man—Brian—responded with a smile. "Mistook him for you, at first." Then he indicated David's feline head. "When he started nuzzling me, I noticed the stripes around his eyes were different. Then I noticed his spot configuration."

Bailey's eyes widened. "David . . . *nuzzled* you?"

Brian shrugged. "Yeah." He rubbed the back of his neck as he glanced from Bailey to David and back again. "Uh, is rubbing not a cat thing?"

"Uh, well." Bailey paused and frowned. "Not on strangers." Then he cocked his head and muttered, "Usually."

"Uh, okay," Brian replied, scratching at his beard. "Maybe he was beggin' for a burger?" Smiling crookedly at David, Brian asked, "You hungry, man?"

Bailey rubbed a palm over his mouth as he eyed David, his eyes narrowing in obvious speculation. "Shift, please, David," he urged.

While it sounded like a request, David knew better. His cat

let out a soft chuff, having enjoyed the human's easy acceptance of their mate.

Mate? David's brain froze as his cat mentally whispered the word.

Yes, mate. His cat was insistent.

Then the animal released his control, and David's form began to change. His muscles popped as his bones realigned. His skin prickled as his fur receded. When he felt pressure behind his eyes, he knew his head was reshaping.

David breathed through the odd sensations, focusing on the end result—his human form.

The feel of a breeze over his flesh reminded David that he was nude and crouching on the wood floor of some stranger's cabin.

Brian, his cat reminded helpfully.

Our mate.

Blowing out a breath, David girded up his courage.

I just found my mate. What if he doesn't like me? Wait? Is he going to expect to fuck me, too?

David's father's angry voice roared through his mind—*A man does the fucking. You gonna be a bitch, boy*—and he did his best to hide his flinch upon the memory of the man's backhand across his face.

"David?" Bailey crouched next to him as he touched his shoulder. "You okay? Lightheaded from running and shifting?" His hand squeezed a little, the touch feeling reassuring. "Take a few even breaths. Then talk to me."

Making a slight nod, David did as he'd been instructed. He focused on the hard floor beneath his palms and breathed slowly. The wood beneath him was faded and scuffed from time and use, but it was clean.

"Is he okay?" Brian asked softly, his deep voice holding a wealth of concern. "I thought you said it doesn't truly hurt to shift, even though it sure as hell sounds like it does."

"Eh. For the most part," Bailey replied. "Shifting is like

working a muscle group," he explained. "If you don't use the muscle, then try to work it hard, it hurts a bit."

"I'm fine," David whispered, knowing he had to explain but fearing it all at the same time. "I just—" He looked toward Bailey and admitted, "He's my mate. I scented him, and I couldn't stop myself from tracking him down. I—"

"Oh," Bailey whispered, his brows slowly drawing together. "Well, that's a good thing," he told him. "Finding your mate, it's a gift from Fate." Evidently, Bailey recognized—or scented—David's fear, for he softly asked, "I know you're bisexual, so why is this such a problem for you?"

David winced, returning his attention to the floor. Embarrassment flooded him as he recalled how his teammates had found out about his bisexuality. For the longest time, he hadn't remembered . . . and then he had.

I wished I hadn't recalled those memories. Some things are better left forgotten.

When the scientists had experimented on David and his teammates, they'd essentially hidden their memories through chemical manipulation. The vampire, Nereo, had arrived at Alpha Declan's request to help clear that blockage. Each session hurt like hell, but David would remember a little more each time.

During one of those sessions, David had recalled his father's abuse upon finding out that David was bisexual. He'd beaten it into his head that fucking a guy was fine, as long as he never accepted the guy's dick into his body. As long as he topped, he was still a man.

As fucked up as David knew it was, that had been the motto he'd lived by. Only one man had ever caused him to question it—fellow teammate, Crew. Except, Crew had been straight as an arrow . . . until he'd met his own mate, Anthony.

Scenting spent seed on Crew's skin had sent David over

the edge. He'd stated some bigoted drivel he didn't even believe in, verbally attacking Crew. Some of the others had arrived, expressing their disgust with David, until Nereo had forced him to explain . . . everything.

While it had been a humiliating experience, his teammates had understood. In time, even Crew had forgiven him. Although, seeing him with his mate still hurt.

Will it hurt now that I've found my own mate?

"I'm sorry," Brian rumbled in his deep, riveting voice. "Did you just say I'm your mate?"

Just that fast, any thoughts of Crew — or hell, anyone from his past — disappeared from David's mind. Jerking his focus from Bailey, he peered up, seeing the questioning look not only in Brian's deep brown eyes, but in his features, as well. The gray in the human's beard and short brown hair didn't detract from his rugged handsomeness — not one bit. In fact, David thought those attributes made him so much sexier.

Good god, did I just think that?

"Uh, yeah," Bailey answered for him.

That was probably good because now that David was focusing on the big muscular man, he couldn't seem to get his mouth to work.

Oh, god. Look at those defined pectorals . . . and his arms . . . how would they feel holding me close? What would his calloused hands feel like against my skin? My cock? I bet —

"Hey, come back to us, David," Bailey urged, snapping his fingers in front of his face. "Come on, buddy. I know the mate-pull can be all-encompassing, but you need to talk to us."

With a deep sigh, Brian muttered, "I'll get you both sweats."

Then the human turned away and started moving toward a chest that was pushed along the wall.

Upon seeing the flex of Brian's back muscles as well as the way his cargo pants cupped his ass, David let out a soft moan. He couldn't help reaching down and pressing the heel of his hand against the base of his suddenly throbbing prick. A shudder of need rocked him to the core.

"Okay, David." Bailey gripped his upper arms. "Let's get you to your feet and out of the cabin."

David curled his lip instinctively, snarling at the other man.

Bailey rolled his eyes, and his grip became more insistent. "I'm not taking you away from Brian, ya dipshit," he muttered, helping David to his feet. "This cabin is saturated in the man's scent. I'm just helping you get some fresh air." A bit louder, Bailey called, "Bring those sweats to the deck. Would ya?"

"Sure, buddy," Brian replied back. Then he groaned and admitted, "I was going to do laundry tomorrow. I only have one pair of clean sweats."

"Whatever shorts you wore to sleep last night will be fine." The words were out of David's mouth before he could censor them.

Holy shit. I can't believe I blurted that.

"Uh, okay. That's a pair of sweat shorts." As Bailey helped David out of the cabin, he heard the man move around the room behind him as he continued, "I'd planned to wear them again tonight, so they're not too bad."

"Come on," Bailey muttered, urging him out the back door.

When a deep whiff of fresh air filled David's lungs, he felt his ardor cool a little. That was followed by a fresh wave of embarrassment. He couldn't believe he'd behaved that way.

"Oh, god," David muttered, grimacing and shaking his head. Staring balefully up at Bailey, he asked, "Was this how you felt when you met Clayton?"

Clayton was Bailey's nerdy human, not that David would ever say that to either man's face. After all, while Clayton's skinny, five-foot-seven frame would label him solidly in the category of twink, Clayton was also a munitions expert. For a number of years, the man had made bombs for a living while his older brother—an ex-Swedish-military sniper—had moved them.

"Yes," Bailey admitted. "One-hundred percent." With a smirk, he guided David to the single step that led off the deck to the grass and urged him to settle on it. "I met my Clayton while in cat form, too." Bailey plopped down beside him and rested his forearms on his knees, completely unmindful of the fact that they were both naked. He stared out at the forest around them, a wry smile curving his lips, as he admitted, "I damn near molested the guy." With a shake of his head, Bailey grimaced and muttered, "Fortunately, Clayton knew more than I did about shifters at that point, so he knew what was happening between us, and he was more than happy with it."

Shrugging, Bailey turned to meet his gaze, rocking his shoulder into David's own as he finished, "I was damn lucky. So damn lucky."

"So . . . me about ready to pounce on the guy, stranger or not, is normal?"

Bailey nodded.

David frowned. "What if we don't even like each other?" He couldn't wrap his brain around the fact that he wanted the other guy so damn badly, even though he knew absolutely nothing about the man. "What if he doesn't bottom?" Lowering his voice, he whispered, "I told you what my father said to me and some of what he did, but not all of it." His heart pounded in his chest as memories better left forgotten assaulted him. David could barely get words out of his thick throat as he whispered roughly, "What if he expects me to bottom?"

"Yeah, I bottom." Brian's deep voice cut into the conversation, revealing that he'd heard them. "For the right man." Squatting behind them, he held out a pair of sweats to Bailey and some shorts to David. "Guess the question is, do you think that you're that right man?"

Even as David's cat yowled in his mind, urging him to declare that yes, they were that man, David couldn't do it. As he held the shorts over his groin, he half-turned to face Brian. "I have issues."

"We all have issues," Brian countered with a shrug.

Wincing, David sucked in a deep breath. Oddly enough, the fact that it was once again laced with Brian's delicious aroma seemed to calm his racing pulse. His dick, which had softened once his nerves had set in, began to plump anew.

Still, David knew he needed to be honest with the guy.

Peering into Brian's deep brown eyes, David admitted, "When my dad found out I was bisexual, he, uh . . . he did stuff to me." David's cheeks flamed, heat rolling through his body for a reason that had nothing to do with arousal. Knowing he had to get it out, he murmured roughly, "He showed me why I never wanted to have anything up my ass."

For several long seconds, only bird-song filled the air.

David's gut clenched.

He wondered how he could feel so miserable on such a gorgeous day.

"Your father sexually abused you?"

When Brian stated the words, bald and to the point, David wanted to snarl at the man. He wanted to deny it. Except, he couldn't.

Peering over his shoulder, David met Brian's solemn gaze and could only whisper one word. "Yeah."

CHAPTER THREE

It took every scrap of self-control Brian could muster to keep his expression neutral. Inside, he seethed. Still, Brian managed to keep his breathing even as he took in David's slumped shoulders and wary expression, knowing he needed to keep his scent under control, too.

Brian wasn't certain that was a thing, but he did his damnedest.

If I ever meet David's father, I will happily snap his neck. Day or night, dark alley or not, I will find a way to murder him without remorse.

Huh. Are these protective instincts caused by that mate-pull shit Bailey and Ronan explained to me? So very strange.

Brian couldn't remember the last time he'd felt so protective of someone. He'd been an only child, and his parents had died young. His grandfather had raised him. While his gramps had been a fair man, he'd been stern, too—ex-military—and Brian had followed in the man's footsteps and joined the marines. His gramps had passed while he'd been on his second tour, but from his letters—the man didn't like computers—Brian had known he'd been proud of him. His gramps had even known he was bisexual, and while it hadn't mattered to him, he had warned Brian to be careful.

When Bailey sighed deeply and murmured, "I'm sorry to hear that, David," Brian yanked his thoughts from his own past. Bailey rested a hand on David's shoulder as he said, "There's an amazing shifter psychiatrist in Stone Ridge, if you ever decide you want to talk about it."

For an instant, David curled his lip and glared at Bailey. He opened his mouth as if he planned to blast him with vitriol. Then his countenance appeared to crumble.

Staring at the ground, David muttered, "I know you mean well when you say that, but I don't need help." His knuckles turned white where they clutched the sweat shorts against his groin. "Real men don't need that shit."

"Another quote from your asshole father," Brian growled out, unable to keep his mouth shut. "I went to a psychiatrist when I was coming to grips with being discharged from the military due to injury." When David snapped his head up and stared at him with wide eyes, Brian knew he'd surprised him. "Does it make me less of a man that I figured out how to process and express my feelings?"

Hell, just because he was a reclusive bastard that didn't like most people, he knew how to understand how he felt about shit.

"I, uh . . ." David snapped his mouth shut, opened it, then closed it again, clearly at a loss for words.

Brian didn't feel the need to make him struggle. Instead, he gave the other man a reassuring smile and used his chin to indicate the shorts. "Why don't you put those on and come back inside?" His stomach rumbled, reminding him of his need for food. "I'm ready to eat. I made three cheeseburger patties." Brian cut a glance Bailey's way, so the other guy knew he was included when Brian returned his attention to David and stated, "You're welcome to join me. It'll give us a chance to talk."

As much as his hard dick would love to skip the talking part, Brian knew that wasn't the best idea. The man who would most likely become his lover — judging by the behavior of other mated pairs he'd heard and seen — clearly needed a soothing hand. Brian knew he could be that guy, although it'd

been a hell of a long time since he'd bothered wooing anyone — man or woman.

"That sounds good, Brian," Bailey immediately replied before focusing on David. "That okay with you, David?"

David hesitated a heartbeat. Then he nodded just a little.

Once Brian received that confirmation, he rested his right
hand on his good thigh. He grunted softly as he rose to a
standing position. Brian turned and took a limping step toward the cabin's back door, feeling his left leg twinge a
smidge. With a shake of his head, he kept moving, easing the
discomfort, all the while knowing he would need to take a little time to heat his muscle at the end of the day.

"Are you okay?" David asked, having obviously noticed
his movements. "What's wrong?"

Brian cast a wry smile over his shoulder as he stated, "Just
can't squat like that much anymore. Old — " His words died
in his throat as he took in the man before him . . . who hadn't
yet pulled on the shorts. "Damn."

The guy was six-foot-one of pure muscle. Having no chest
hair, his pectorals were well-defined and on clear display, and
his pink nipples called for Brian's tongue. His abdominals
were sculpted with a well-defined six-pack. Not even a treas-
ure trail marred the gorgeous vee that pointed toward the
man's glorious erection, which jutted from a very lightly
haired groin.

That's gotta be a perfect eight-inch mouthful.

Bailey snapping his fingers in front of his face finally
snapped Brian out of his openly appreciative ogling. He
blinked once before turning toward Bailey, taking in the
man's cheeky grin. With a shrug, Brian returned his attention
to David. He wasn't going to apologize for admiring a sexy
naked man, especially since Fate decided he would be all his.

By then, a clearly blushing David was straightening from
where he'd just finished pulling on the shorts.

Too bad.

Brian met David's pale blue eyes, seeing uncertainty there. The expression seemed at odds with the man's strong jaw and physique. Brian had the urge to skim a hand over David's closely-shorn blond hair to settle at his neck, giving the tight tendons there a massage in an attempt to soothe him.

"Food," Bailey reminded, poking Brian in the ribs.

Blowing out a breath, Brian nodded. "Damn," he muttered as he headed into the cabin. "These urges are intense, even on the human side of it." As he opened not only the fruit salad container but the potato salad one, as well, he mused, "Would never have thought that."

"Fate does like to get her way," Bailey commented as he made himself comfortable in Brian's kitchen, pulling out extra plates and utensils. "Or so I've heard."

Brian grunted.

"Buns?" Bailey asked, peering at his cupboard shelves.

"Uh, no. Sorry," Brian replied. He pointed at the lettuce head on the table. "I wrap mine in lettuce leaves." Seeing Bailey's arched brow, he shrugged and admitted, "When deciding to cut carbs, since I don't work out like I did in the military, bread seemed an easy way to go. These days, I grow most of my own vegetables." Brian pointed to the east. "Huge secluded greenhouse in that direction." Then he pointed at the patties. "And these are venison burgers. Shot and processed the deer myself."

"Okay." Bailey shrugged and joined him at the table.

Brian noticed David lurked just inside the doorway. Smiling, he beckoned. "Please." Leading by example, he settled on one of the straight-backed chairs. "Have a seat and help yourself."

To Brian's pleasure, David obeyed.

David eased onto the chair to Brian's right, then took the plate and silverware Bailey offered him. In companionable silence, they fixed their plates. Seeing the amount of fruit and potato salad that the two shifters heaped onto their plates reminded him of the huge appetites most shifters sported. As David took his first bite of venison cheeseburger, humming appreciatively, he mentally reassessed his food stores capacity.

I'll need to expand it . . . and figure out a way to put in a hydroponics bay.

"This is really good," Bailey mumbled around his mouthful of burger. After he swallowed, he added, "I always forget how hungry shifting and running makes me."

"Oh, good," David murmured, the lines around his blue eyes relaxing just a little. "So, it's not just me."

Bailey shook his head. "No, it's a paranormal thing." After giving him a reassuring grin, he told him, "I hear it's the same for all races."

David's relief seemed a palpable thing, and he began eating faster.

As Brian relaxed back in his chair, he watched the pair take seconds, then thirds, finishing the fruit salad and potato salad. Taking a sip of his water, he realized he hadn't offered either man a drink. Rectifying that, he listed the few beverages he had on hand.

"Just water for me would be great," Bailey replied. "I'll need to be running back soon." Tapping David on the back of his hand with his fork, he asked, "You staying or coming with me?"

"Uh, w-water is fine," David stuttered, glancing between them. "A-And, uh, I-I don't know."

"We can meet again in a neutral setting," Brian offered as he fetched two more bottles of water from his fridge. Placing them on the table and retaking his seat, he used a hand to indicate the clearly intimate space. "I don't want you to feel intimidated, forced, or pressured into thinking we have to do, well, anything."

No matter what my hard dick thinks.

While Brian knew shifters did things fast, David hadn't been born a shifter. He'd been made into one through illegal experimentation. Brian guessed the man was probably damn conflicted about everything.

For a long moment, David sipped his water and remained silent. He frowned at the table. His expression even appeared a little vacant, as if he was having an internal debate with himself.

Hell, for all Brian knew, he was.

Well, having an internal debate with his cat, anyway.

Brian had once asked how that worked. Were shifters always in tune with their animal? Or did they sometimes disagree? Were they two personalities or one?

Alpha Declan had explained that he and his animal were one and the same being. While a wolf, their instincts to care and protect were a wee bit heightened. They could still think and reason while in their animal form, so normally, they were in tune with each other.

From what Brian had understood, only when the human needed to go against their animal's instincts for some reason—for example, not being able to claim their mate first thing, or allowing their mate to go into a dangerous situation—did they end up disagreeing. The stronger the shifter, the more pronounced their need to protect and look after those they cared about.

"Does it, um . . ." David began slowly, as if choosing his words carefully. He paused a second to glance between Bailey and Brian before focusing on Brian. His voice came out surprisingly soft, betraying his unease, when he asked, "Does it make me seem like a girl if I want to go on a date first?"

"Not at all." Brian was quick to reassure David. After a second of his own hesitation, he reached over and placed his palm over David's wrist as he said, "I'm actually flattered."

After staring at where Brian touched him for a few seconds, David lifted his chin and met Brian's gaze. "You are?"

Brian smiled. "Oh, yes." He squeezed David's wrist lightly while rubbing his thumb over the back of the man's hand, enjoying the feel of his skin. "You see, it means you care about the man I am, as a person." With a smirk, Brian continued, "I've been around shifters for a while now, and I know they do things fast. Meet your mate and bam." He snapped his fingers. "Bond. Then get to know that person and figure out how to mesh their lives." Brian shrugged. "And there's nothing wrong with that, but neither of us are shifters." When Bailey opened his mouth as if to counter him, Brian held up his free hand, stalling the other man's words. "David didn't start out as a shifter. Up here"—he tapped the side of his head—"he still thinks like a human." Returning his focus to David's blue eyes, appreciating the relief he found within their depths, Brian asked, "So, how about I pick you up for dinner this evening? We'll go to Stone Ridge for a meal. I hear Caribou's is delicious, and I haven't tried it, yet."

Rarely did Brian patron a restaurant. Having been in the military, he found himself constantly assessing everything—from mapping the swiftest exits to the expressions of every person in the place for motive. It was a stressful and uncomfortable situation for him.

Except, for David, Brian was willing to put himself through it.

Huh. Probably part of the mate-pull thing, too.

"Thank you for understanding. I appreciate it."

David turned his hand and clasped Brian's hand fully.

The move caused the hairs on Brian's arm to stand on end. Warmth traveled up his limb, heating him from the inside out. As his dick twitched behind his fly, butterflies began to dance in his belly.

Okay. This is weird.

Brian could only liken the experience to holding hands with a crush.

Doing his best to control the sudden pounding of his heart

and the way sweat beaded on the back of his neck, Brian asked, "Can I pick you up at . . . uh . . . wherever you're staying at around" — he glanced over his shoulder at the battery-powered clock on the wall — "seven-thirty this evening?"

That would give him a few hours to finish most of his afternoon's *to do* list.

"Yeah," David agreed before licking his bottom lip. "And I'm staying at Ronan and Markus's right now."

That surprised Brian. "You're not at Declan's with the others?" He'd heard that was where they were all rehabilitating, but he hadn't wanted to make assumptions.

David shook his head, his brows furrowing and his expression pinching. "I couldn't stay there after . . ." Grimacing, he lowered his attention to the table. "Well, after Crew hooked up with Anthony and I got most of my memories back." His voice turned hoarse as he whispered, "Too many memories."

Brian figured there was a story there, but he wouldn't press. Instead, he couldn't help but ask, "How come you're not staying with Bailey?"

Bailey scoffed. "I live with Clayton over his shop," he explained. "It's a one-bedroom, although I did offer our sofa." Smirking, he told him, "Ronan and Markus have a guest bedroom. Much more comfortable."

Chuckling, Brian nodded. "Makes sense." Squeezing David's hand once more, he confirmed, "So, I'll see you at seven-thirty at Ronan's."

David nodded. "Seven-thirty." He squeezed Brian's hand back.

Taking their lunch together as a good sign that David was beginning to be able to express himself a little, Brian eased his grip and stood. "I look forward to it." Then Brian began clearing the table, putting away condiments, and filling the sink with sudsy water to wash everything up.

Bailey rose, too, lending a hand.

David remained at the table, as if frozen.

While Bailey wiped down the table, he asked, "David, are you okay?"

Bailey spoke the question so softly that Brian almost missed it. He shut off the water and paused, peering in their direction. Taking in the way David gripped his knees with his hands caused concern to bloom within Brian's chest, and he moved toward them.

Lifting his gaze from where he stared at the table, David admitted, "I'm not certain I'll be able to get my cheetah to run home with you." His blue eyes held a wealth of confusion mixed with frustration. "How the hell do you control it?"

Bailey rested his hand on David's in reassurance. "Come out back with me," he urged. "I'll walk you through it, and me and my cat will help get you moving."

David rose, and Bailey guided him toward the door.

When Brian began to follow, Bailey held up a hand. "It'd be better if you stayed in here until David gets his cat under control and we're gone."

Brian nodded once. "Okay."

"And please close the windows and doors," Bailey instructed.

"See you later, David," Brian assured even as he did as Bailey had ordered.

"See you," David replied, sounding a little dazed.

After Brian closed the doors and window, he crossed to the kitchen and watched as two cheetahs, one clearly reluctant, disappeared into the forest.

Well, hell. Guess Fate decided to meddle in my life some more.

As Brian gathered everything that he would need to put up the surveillance cameras, he thought about David, and he couldn't say he minded so much.

CHAPTER FOUR

David settled on a sofa in the front room and tapped his fingers on his thigh. A moment later, he bounced back to his feet and began pacing . . . again. He couldn't seem to stay still.

Between his nerves as he thought about going on a date with a man as well as his cat's annoyance that they'd left their unclaimed mate deep in the forest, all alone, he felt as if he was going to jump right out of his skin.

Or shift and go hunt down said mate.

While David knew he'd still been learning to co-exist with the new voice inside his head, nothing could have prepared him for the onslaught of need he'd felt upon scenting, then meeting, Brian Haas.

"Damn, buddy." Markus strode down the stairs, eyeing him. "You look about as nervous as a cat in a room full of rocking chairs."

David paused, processing that comment. As he imagined it, he shook his head. "Poor cat," he muttered without missing a step.

Markus scoffed. "Yeah. Poor cat." Stopping beside the sofa, he rested one hip against it as he crossed his arms over his chest. He cocked his head in a quizzical way — or a very canine way, considering he was a wolf shifter. "So, your mate is coming to pick you up iiiiinnnn" — he glanced toward a wall clock with a depiction of a wolf howling at a full moon on it — "any minute now. What's eating you?"

"I want him, and yet I don't," David blurted out. Instantly, his face felt as if it was on fire.

"Ooookay." Markus moved to sit on the sofa. Leaning forward, he rested his forearms on his knees and clasped his hands together. With narrowed eyes, he asked, "Care to explain that?"

"Not really," David grumbled. Still, he knew he couldn't put the man off. He'd been nice enough to open his home to David, and he'd been nothing but kind and supportive as he helped him come to terms with essentially having an unknown psyche awaken in his mind. David plopped onto the chair to the sofa's left and rubbed his palms over his thighs. "This voice in my head is chanting mate, mate, mate and mine, mine, mine. I'm attracted to the man, but I'm scared to death to do anything about it." Staring pensively at Markus, David admitted, "While in human form, I wanna do things to him. Uh, kiss and hold hands and touch and shit. As a cat, I want to mark him. Lick him, rub against him, cover him in my scent." Grimacing, David finished on a whisper, "Bite him."

Markus arched one brow. "You want to bite him while you're a cheetah?"

"Yes. No." David frowned at the floor. "I don't know." Meeting Markus's gaze again, he lifted a hand and used a finger to make a whirling motion next to his head. "It's all mixed up up here."

"Okay, let's start with the biting thing then." Markus offered him an encouraging smile. "Your cat recognized him as your mate even before you did. I can guarantee that he doesn't want to bite and hurt him."

"You sure?" David rubbed the back of his neck. "Cause it'd just about kill me if I accidentally hurt him."

"I'm sure," Markus responded, sounding so damn certain that some of David's nerves began to ebb. Smiling at him, Markus told him, "The desire to bite is your cat urging you to claim him as your mate. To bond with him." Furrowing his brows, Markus asked, "Has someone explained how to bond with your mate? Or did we miss that?"

Grunting, David bounced back to his feet and began pacing again. "Yeah, yeah," he mumbled, doing his best to fight down the embarrassed blush that threatened to rise up his neck. "Uh, you fuck your mate, spill in his or her body, and bite them." David pivoted and began crossing the large living space once more. "Why the hell would a shifter want to bite his mate if he's supposed to want to please and care for him?" He scrubbed his palm over his close-cropped scalp. "It makes no damn sense."

"Ah, that's what we missed," Markus mused, rising and moving into David's path. "David. Stop for a minute." He rested his palms on David's shoulders, then moved one hand to his nape and began massaging rhythmically. "Just relax, and focus on me."

To David's surprise, he felt his tension receding. His cat calmed in his mind. He peered into Markus's hazel eyes, seeing nothing but warmth and understanding within their depths.

"There's nothing wrong with your desires," Markus assured him with a smile. "When you bite your mate, it'll make him orgasm. He will *love* it."

Gaping, David stared at the other man for one heartbeat, two, before he managed to snap his jaw closed. "I-I'm sorry. What did you say?"

The sound of a vehicle approaching reached David's ears, and a fresh wave of nerves fired through him.

"You heard me," Markus replied, releasing him in favor of moving toward the door. Walking backward, he hollered, "Hey, Ronan?"

"Yeah, babe?" The thickly built, ex-marine appeared at the head of the stairs. "You need something?"

David knew Ronan had once been on a team with Brian, so

he figured they were around the same age—in the neighbor-hood of fifty. While his mate sported a thick, gray and brown beard and hair, giving him a wild, mountain man appearance, Ronan kept his hair similar to David's—shorn close to his scalp and clean-shaven. His dark eyes glittered with una-bashed interest as he stared down at Markus, clearly comfort-able with his desire for the wolf shifter.

Markus grinned up at him, his hazel eyes twinkling with mischief. "Do you orgasm when I bite you?"

Growling loudly, Ronan's smile turned feral. "Hell yeah, I do." He smirked. "You hankerin' for some fun while David's on his date?"

Groaning, Markus reached down and adjusted his clearly defined hard-on behind the fly of his jeans. "Well, now that you mention it."

David sucked in a shocked gasp as a wealth of arousal and pheromones flooded the huge room, and discomfort filled him, since he now knew exactly what they would be doing while he was out.

Holy shit.

The doorbell drew David's attention, and instinct had him starting toward the door.

Considering Markus had already been halfway there, it wasn't a surprise when he beat David to it. The wolf shifter swung the door wide and greeted Brian. Markus didn't invite him in, however.

"It's good to see you again, Brian," Markus told David's human, lifting his hand to keep him on the doorstep. "I don't mean to be rude, but I need ya to take David and go." He glanced over his shoulder, peering up the stairs as he growled huskily, "Got me a date with my man."

Brian snorted, not seeming to be put out in the least bit. "Having David in the house crampin' your style, Markus?" he teased.

"Naw, we fuck several times a day," Markus replied, not

in the least bit shy in talking about his sex life. "But I was telling David about how his claiming bite will make you orgasm, had Ronan confirm it, and now . . . I got me a boner I wanna satisfy."

Brian snorted. "Charmer."

"Yep," Markus quipped right back.

Peering past Markus, Brian locked his dark-eyed gaze on David and smiled at him. "You ready to go, David?"

Too shocked at their blatant confidence and comfort in discussing male on male sex, David couldn't find his tongue, so he just nodded.

Lifting his hand, palm up, Brian wiggled his fingers, urging him forward. "All right then." He swept his gaze over David boldly. "You look great. You need a jacket?"

David glanced down at himself. He was only wearing jeans and a long-sleeved button-down top, but he supposed it did mold well to his muscular form. In truth, David had been too keyed up to really pay attention to what Ronan had left out on the bed and practically ordered him to wear.

Huh. I do look pretty good.

"David?" Brian touched David's upper arm, surprising David that he'd already reached the door. The other man stared down the couple of inches in height he had on David and repeated, "Jacket?"

Even feeling completely overwhelmed, David shook his head. "Uh, run hotter these days."

Brian nodded. "Gotcha. Heard that about shifters." Then he settled his broad hand on David's back and began guiding him off the porch and toward his truck. "How about we get out of their hair and get started on our own date?"

David once again followed along. "Okay."

Finally, when Brian opened the passenger side door for him, David felt yanked out of whatever headspace he'd been caught in. "Uh." Narrowing his eyes, he glanced from Brian to the open door and back again. "You know I'm not the girl in this relationship, right?"

Upon hearing the defensiveness and even irritation in his tone, David almost winced.

Shit.

Brian didn't seem fazed at all, however. Instead, he smirked and swept his gaze over David in a slow and appreciative — *very* slow and appreciative — once over.

"Oh, David," Brian rumbled, his voice dropping deep. "I *know* you're not a girl." Then he met David's eyes as he solemnly stated, "Just as *I* am not a girl."

Confusion replaced David's rising ire. "Then, what's with the door?" He pointed as if he needed to add emphasis.

"David, I picked you up, so I'm being respectful of my date," Brian told him, clearly confident in his actions. "I would expect you to do the same for me."

"Soooo, if we were just going to the grocery store, would you still open my door for me?" David couldn't seem to let it go.

"Depends on whose car we took."

Confused by the answer, David didn't resist when Brian gently gripped his hand and urged him toward the cab. He was up and buckled in, the door shut behind him and Brian striding around the front, when he processed the comment. He watched Brian climb inside and shut the door, but he held his tongue until after Brian had started the truck and began them moving.

"What do you mean it depends on whose car? What's that mean?"

"Way back when, I was raised by my grandfather. Gramps taught me that a man opens the door for his date," Brian told him, turning the truck onto the winding mountain road, heading toward town. "When I came out, explaining that I was bisexual, so sometimes my dates were men and it was a moot point, Gramps scowled at me and shook his head."

"Damn," David whispered. "He didn't approve?"

I know how that feels.

To David's surprise, Brian barked a laugh, a wide grin curving his bearded lips. "Oh, he didn't give a shit about that." He lifted a hand and waved negligently. "No," Brian continued. "No, he told me that even if my date was a man, I still needed to treat him with respect, just as I should expect my male date to treat me with respect in return."

"Wow, really?"

How would it be to have a parent . . . or grandparent . . . be that accepting?

David did his best to squelch his gut-churning sensation of jealousy.

"Really," Brian continued, seemingly ignorant of David's uncomfortable response — *thank god.* "Of course, me being the ignorant young fool that I was, I asked what Gramps was talking about." Scoffing, Brian glanced David's way, a wry smile curving his lips. "After all, guys don't need respect from their dates, right? We're men. We're macho. We can handle anything."

Exactly.

David just managed to keep from saying that out loud, for which he was grateful. Especially when Brian continued his explanation.

"Wrong, my gramps told me," Brian stated. A fond smile curved his lips, and he was clearly recalling the conversation with happiness. "My gramps explained that for any relationship to work, it had to first begin on a solid foundation of respect and trust. Sure, attraction needs to be there, too" — Brian glanced David's way and gave him a heated smile before returning his focus to the road — "but what good is that if you can't trust your partner?"

Nodding slowly, David mused, "Okay. I can understand that."

"Anyway." Brian barked a quiet laugh. "What I mean by my longwinded explanation is that, if I'm driving, I respect you enough to open your car door, even if it's as something as simple as grocery shopping." Stopping at a four-way stop sign, he pinned a serious look on David. "But that goes both ways. If you picked up a girl in your vehicle for a date, wouldn't you open the door for her?"

"Of course," David instantly responded. Then it hit him what Brian was getting at. "It's a sign of my respect for my date. That means I should do that same to a guy I was dating, too."

Brian dipped his chin in a silent nod before glancing both ways and starting them forward.

After a moment of silence, where David mulled that over, he took a chance and reached out to Brian. He rested his hand over the man's thick wrist even as his hand gripped the wheel. When Brian glanced his way, David smiled at him.

"Thank you for explaining that to me, Brian," David told him softly. "I appreciate it. I—" He hesitated an instant before admitting, "I sure as hell never would have considered it that way before."

Hell, everything Brian's gramps had instilled in him was the exact opposite of what David's father had beaten into him. Of the two, David had to believe that Gramps was the one in the right on the matter.

Brian released the wheel with his left hand and laid it over David's. "You're welcome," he replied, squeezing softly before returning his hand to the wheel.

His head churning with his thoughts, David returned his hand to his lap. He stared out the window and tried to process this new turn of events for him.

Could he be the man Brian so obviously deserved?

David didn't know, but he sure would like the chance to give it his best shot.

CHAPTER FIVE

When David lapsed into silence, Brian worried for a few minutes. After a couple of glances his date's way, that tension eased. He saw the contemplative expression on the man's face and realized he must have given David quite a bit to think about.

Brian wondered about David's teen years . . . and he didn't. Just the hints were enough to turn his stomach. He wondered if the teen version of David had had anyone to turn to in his time of need. Brian worried that he hadn't.

Maybe someday, we'll have the kind of relationship where I could ask him.

This was not that day, however.

Spotting the sign that read, *Welcome to Stone Ridge*, Brian wondered if the note at the bottom stating, *Population 1,487* was accurate. He had a funny feeling it wasn't. It wouldn't surprise him to discover that Alpha Declan was savvy enough to hide the town's actual population from the government.

Never can be too careful.

As more homes began popping up left and right, Brian noticed David rouse from whatever thoughts had consumed him. He began to look left and right. David appeared to be interested in everything, taking in the sights as swiftly as he could.

Wondering about the man—altered man—who Fate had deemed the other half of his soul—*never would that thought have entered my mind just over a year ago*—Brian asked, "Have you ever been to Caribou's?" Brian recalled mentioning that he had not, but David hadn't really said.

David immediately shook his head. "I haven't been to town before," he admitted. Glancing left and right, he murmured, "It's like a quaint little forest town a kid would see in picture books." David hesitated, glancing his way while an expression of embarrassment tightened his cheeks, and he quickly added, "The sidewalks look clean, and the storefronts are old but in nice shape, obviously cared for."

Brian looked around, trying to see it from David's perspective. His date was right. The storefronts had fresh-looking advertisements and were clear of clutter. A few places even had fresh coats of paint.

Even at nearly eight o'clock at night on a weekday, there were a number of people milling along the roads, smiling and chatting with each other.

Good Lord. How about that. It does look like something out of a picture book.

Glancing over everyone quickly, Brian absently wondered how many of those people were shifters.

Hell, maybe they're something else.

While Alpha Declan hadn't specifically mentioned many other species in his town, that didn't mean they weren't there. The wolf alpha seemed to be an accepting sort. He wanted peace, but he seemed to be happy to back that up with force, too.

Manages a good balance as far as I've seen and considering the help he's offered me for my project.

"You're right," Brian commented, seeing the vulnerable expression taking over David's features, regardless of how much he tried to hide it. "I've been told only good things about living here." Waving his hand to indicate the sheriff's station, Brian scoffed. "Except for the asshole sheriff, but at least that's changed recently."

"Yeah, with the arrival of *Anthony*," David grumbled as he narrowed his eyes at the indicated building.

"Uh, you have something against Anthony?" Brian asked softly, noting the guy's intonation.

Does David have a problem with authority figures after everything he sent through?

That could cause problems living as a shifter in a pack . . . pride . . . whatever.

Just as quickly, David's posture deflated. "No," he muttered, sounding somewhat forlorn. "Just . . . memories I wished I hadn't remembered dredging up emotions I would rather not recall. I—" David peered his way out of the corner of his eye, his lips pinched in frustration. "I'm sorry."

Brian spotted the sign for Caribou's Bar and Grill even as he lifted his shoulders in a shrug. "You don't have to apologize to me." As he guided his truck into a parking spot, he added, "Hell, I don't even know what you're saying sorry for." Once Brian had thrown the vehicle into park, he turned to face David. "If you want to talk about it, I'm here for you. If you don't, that's fine, too." He sobered as he added the caveat, "However, if it continues to create mood swings, I'll probably urge you to get help for whatever's bothering you. You already know I believe in therapy."

David stared at him with wide blue eyes. His mouth opened and closed for a second. Then he furrowed his brows as he slowly began to nod.

"Fair enough," David mumbled, then winced as he glanced toward the restaurant. "I'm willing to share a little over a beer . . . if that's okay with you."

"Sounds just fine with me," Brian agreed.

The smile Brian received made him feel about ten feet tall. *Just damn.*

Brian shut off the engine and pulled his keys from the ignition. After he'd slipped from the vehicle, noting David had followed his lead, he shut his door and locked it. When they reached the front door, Brian couldn't resist reaching past David and opening the door for him.

He ignored the arched brow David cast his way and relished the pleasure he felt at causing the hint of a smile that toyed around the man's lips.

Reaching the hostess stand, Brian responded to the usual questions. No, he didn't have a reservation. He would prefer a table.

She led them to the right side of the restaurant and set them up at a square, four-person table. Even though the woman placed the menus across from each other, he waited until David had chosen his seat. Then he sat to the shifter's left.

Brian knew that proximity and touch were key to their species. While David's brain still seemed to be stuck in the human mindset, he knew there were shifter genetics in there, too. He needed to soothe both, to connect with both, not only in order for David to settle, but for their connection to progress.

No relationship is all about sex . . . as much as I'd love to fuck the handsome man or have him fuck me. Can't bone all the time.

Pushing those thoughts aside—it wasn't as if they were doing his half-hard dick any good—Brian focused on the menu. He noticed the place had the standard steakhouse fare. What he found interesting were the options to get not only sixteen-ounce steaks, but twenty-four and thirty-six-ounce sizes, too.

Huh. I wonder if the place is run by a shifter, so he's aware of their increased appetites.

Dismissing the thought, Brian asked, "Do you drink?" He didn't often bother anymore, but a date night was a good reason to enjoy an adult beverage.

"Uh, yeah." David lifted his attention from the menu to peer at him. "Beer mostly."

"Hmmm." Brian nodded, glancing between David and the separate laminated card listing the drinks. "Would you be interested in splitting a bottle of wine with me?" Smiling wryly at the other man, he added, "I don't think this type of place offers pitchers of beer."

"Actually, if you were sitting in the bar area, we do," the waiter countered, announcing his arrival. His smile froze for just a second as his attention was snagged by David. His eyes widened before he seemed to catch himself. After clearing his throat, he stated, "I'm Earl, and I'll be your waiter this evening." With another glance between them, he asked, "Can I start you off with something to drink besides water? Or can I get an appetizer started for you?"

"A bottle of wine is fine, Brian," David cut in, touching his wrist with his forefingers. "I'm partial to white, if that's okay."

Brian nodded. "Sounds good." Then he pointed at a selection he remembered enjoying in the past. "Also, how about an order of your boneless buffalo wings?"

After all, what's a date night without some overindulgence?

Once Earl had left the table, David asked, "Uh, that's going to have breading baked on it, ya know. I thought you don't eat bread." A second later, he quickly added, "Uh, not that I'm accusing you of anything or something. Just . . . you didn't at the cabin and—" With a groan, David muttered, "Shutting up now."

"Normally, I don't," Brian agreed with a soft chuckle, doing his best to reassure David that he wasn't upset by the question. "I don't have bread in the house for a few reasons, but I'm not averse to eating it on occasion." Lifting his attention to David, Brian told him, "Sort of like a treat." He waggled his brows and pointed at the dessert section. "Tonight, I even intend to get this hot fudge lava cake explosion thingy for dessert."

As Brian had hoped, David lowered his gaze to the mentioned item. His eyes widened as he read the description, and he hummed appreciatively.

Lowering his voice in a way he hoped was seductive—Brian hadn't tried to, or needed to, seduce someone in . . . well over a decade—he rumbled, "Split it with ya."

David's attention jerked back to Brian. His nostrils flared as his eyes widened. He even swallowed so hard that his Adam's apple bobbed.

When David whispered, "Okay," his voice came out husky, causing goose bumps to dance across Brian's nerve endings.

Perfect.

Hopefully, David's reaction meant they were both on the same page—interested in seeing where a little after-date fun might lead.

Then Brian spotted the slight flush darkening David's cheeks and the way he dipped his head in embarrassment.

Patience.

Lowering his attention to the menu, Brian asked, "Anything calling your name?"

David lifted his shoulders in a small shrug. "Well, I know this is a steakhouse, but Ronan and Markus grill a lot of those at home, so . . ." His brows furrowed as he swept his attention over the selections.

In truth, Brian grilled a lot, too. While he had an oven, he didn't bake much. He used it mainly for when he had a hankerin' for a pizza, which wasn't all that often because he had to make the dough from scratch. It was a good thing that pepperoni lasted for months at a time in the refrigerator.

"I'm looking at the shrimp linguini," Brian told his date, casting a wry grin David's way as he leaned closer to the man. Lowering his voice, he admitted, "It's been a few years since I went to a restaurant, David, and I can't remember the last time I had a pasta dish I didn't make using spaghetti squash as the noodles."

"Spaghetti squash?" David whispered, his attention snagging on Brian's lips.

Brian barely refrained from acting on that subconscious invitation.

Oh, wow. If only we weren't in a restaurant.

Instead, Brian nodded. "Yeah. I grow them in my greenhouse. Cut them in half, steam them in water, and peel out the inside," he explained as he slowly straightened. "They work just as well, taste great, and are low in carbs."

Just then, Earl returned with the wine. After he opened it and poured a little into a glass, he glanced between them. "Who would like to try it?"

"I already know I like it." Brian indicated David. "Try a sip. Tell me what you think."

David did as he'd been bidden. After a couple of sips, he stated, "It's good." With a nod, he smiled at Brian. "Good choice."

As Earl poured their drinks, he asked, "Have you decided on your meals, or do you still need a few minutes?"

"I have," Brian confirmed. Arching a brow, he focused on David. "What about you?"

David nodded again. "Yeah. I'm ready."

Brian put in his order for the shrimp linguini dish, adding a side salad with extra vinaigrette dressing. David ordered the fish and chips meal with a side of macaroni and cheese. Unable to help himself, Brian quickly added a side lobster tail, too.

Earl grinned. "Good choices all around." The man cast another quick glance David's way before adding, "I'll get these put in, and I'm sure your appetizer will be up soon." Then Earl hurried off.

Shaking his head, Brian muttered, "Earl keeps looking at you." He narrowed his eyes as a kernel of jealousy flared to life within him. "I know I'm older than you, but it's still a little rude for him to be checking you out when you're obviously here with me."

David's attention snapped to Brian over the rim of his wine glass. He'd just taken a sip, and he gulped quickly. Then he coughed once as he set his wine down and grabbed his napkin. Lifting it to his mouth, David coughed a few more times.

Brian grimaced, pushing David's water glass closer to him. "Sorry."

Shaking his head before taking several swallows of water, David actually appeared to be smiling around the rim as he drank. He finally seemed to get ahold of himself. When David lowered the cup to the table, he was definitely grinning.

"Earl wasn't checking me out," David murmured. He even reached over and placed his hand over Brian's, as if it was his turn to be reassuring. Lowering his voice even more, David told him, "Earl is a wolf shifter. He's probably trying to figure out what the hell I am."

"What do you mean?" Brian really should have considered that.

David winced, leaning closer. "I don't smell . . . *right*."

"Right?"

Nodding, David explained, "He can scent that I'm a cat shifter, but I've been told that those of us who were . . . altered . . . have a distinct odor to us that sets us apart." He straightened as he finished, "The random shifter probably wouldn't be able to place it, and it would confuse their senses a little."

"Ah." Brian hummed, furrowing his brows as he took a sip of his wine. Concern filled him as thoughts ran rampant. "He's not a danger to you, is he?"

David quickly shook his head. "No. Not at all."

"You sure?" Brian never wanted to put the other man in harm's way. He'd been through enough already.

"I'm sure."

Brian had to take David at his word. Besides, the middle of a busy restaurant wasn't the place to get into it. While his date could tell who was what, Brian couldn't . . . not unless he'd already been introduced to them.

Taking a quick glance around the room, Brian realized he only recognized a couple of people in the room. Detective Lyle Sullivan sat eating dinner with his partner, Todd Abernathy. The pair were cuddled in a booth, enjoying a bottle of wine and what appeared to be a half-dozen of the appetizer dishes.

Yum. That's a good idea, too. Skip a meal and get a variety.

Lyle turned his head, meeting his gaze. He dipped his chin in a nod of acknowledgment, then returned to his food.

"They're probably here to make certain I don't accidentally cause a scene."

Returning his attention to David, Brian asked, "What do you mean?"

David's lips were curved in a sardonic smile as he explained, "I'm still getting the hang of being a shifter, so . . . eh." He shrugged. "Just in case I get upset or something, he can talk me down or order me down. Lyle's a damn dominant animal and a hell of a lot bigger than, well, just about all of us."

"Really?" Brian couldn't recall what Lyle shifted into. "Good thing he's loyal to Declan then."

Brian nodded. "Good thing."

Then, blatantly changing the subject, David asked, "So, what keeps you so busy out there in the wilds of the mountains?"

Not minding one bit, Brian began to share his plans for the pack's wilderness retreat.

CHAPTER SIX

David found the conversation flowing easily, alleviating some of his concerns. Having never been on a date with a man, he'd wondered if there would be awkward lulls. To his surprise, he discovered it felt almost like talking with a member of his team.

When Earl brought their appetizer, they paused for a few minutes to enjoy the tasty boneless buffalo wings. Then the conversation picked right back up. Brian shared what he was doing deep in the mountains—building a hideaway for Declan's pack—and David found the concept of doomsday prepping fascinating.

Brian ran everything off the grid. His food preparations were extensive, but after sharing a meal with him and Bailey, he'd decided it wasn't enough. David had always had a green thumb, and he'd offered Brian a hand with figuring out hydroponics, which his mate immediately took him up on.

A burst of pleasure that didn't feel all his own surged through David, and he realized his cat was practically preening in the back of his mind. Evidently, his animal liked the fact that they could contribute to their mate's plans. David appreciated that his offer of support seemed welcome.

Hell, I need something to do with my time these days.

David had been getting bored.

And now, with a mate like Brian, I won't be.

The man's plans were extensive.

Of course, that meant figuring out the whole bonding thing, but David hoped they could get there. His randy dick certainly wanted that, too.

Noticing that Brian had begun slowing his fork-to-mouth movements, David glanced at all the food still before them. His mate had shared his lobster tail with him, so he'd reciprocated by giving his mate several bites of his mac and cheese. They'd also enjoyed sharing each other's entrees, although Brian still had half of his left.

"Are you going to finish your meal?" David asked as he dipped the last bite of his fried cod into a tub of tartar sauce. Then he popped it into his mouth and hummed appreciatively. He couldn't help eyeing Brian's half-finished shrimp linguini. The dish had been divine.

David could honestly say his favorite thing about being a shifter was the increased metabolism. He could eat and drink damn near anything without gaining a pound. Well, within reason, anyway. If he sat on the sofa drinking beer all day, David was certain he would pay for it.

Fortunately, that wasn't the type of person David was. He enjoyed physical activity.

Brian chuckled softly as he leaned back in his chair. "Help yourself," he urged while patting his flat belly. "I've had my fill." With a wink, Brian added, "Gotta save a little room for that dessert, after all."

Unable to resist that offer, David grabbed his last few fries before pushing the basket away. He popped them into his mouth before easing Brian's dish toward him. David sighed with pleasure as he took a bite of the food.

"This is so good," David mumbled around his mouthful. Upon hearing Brian's soft chuckle, he paused and focused on the man. To his surprise, David saw a mixture of pleasure and mirth in his mate's eyes. He wondered from where it stemmed and had to ask, "What?"

Leaning forward, Brian rested his forearms on the table. He cradled his wineglass between his forefingers, pitching his voice low as he admitted, "I really enjoy watching you eat." Brian tipped his head to the side as he asked, "Do you think that's a mate thing?" He waved one hand toward the plethora of empty dishes. "I ordered more than I knew I could eat because I figured you would help me with it, considering" — Brian paused as he made a circular motion of David's body — "what you are now."

"Really? Thank you." David couldn't help but smile at his mate's thoughtfulness. "And I really have no idea. We'd have to ask Declan or Markus."

"How is everything, gentlemen?" Earl asked, stopping beside their table. He began picking up the empty dishes. "Have you saved room for dessert?"

Brian nodded. "Absolutely." He relaxed back in his chair, perhaps to give Earl more room to collect their plates. "We'd like to share one of the molten lava cakes. It sounds delicious."

"That's a definite customer favorite," Earl confided, nodding. "Can't go wrong with it. I'll be back with it soon."

Earl hurried off again. At least the wolf shifter hadn't sniffed at him again.

It hadn't escaped David's notice that Lyle had discreetly motioned the wolf shifter over. Earl had tensed for a moment as the detective had spoken to him. Then his shoulders had sagged, and he'd nodded, appearing relieved.

If David had to guess, Lyle had explained who he was and that he was there with Declan's permission.

"While we wait for dessert, I need to use the men's room," David stated, feeling his bladder twinge.

"Need a hand?" Brian asked, his eyes twinkling and his tone teasing.

Scoffing, David shook his head. "I think I can handle it." He set down his fork and rose to his feet. "Be right back." After taking a couple of steps away from the table, he turned back and pointed at the bowl of Brian's food that he'd been working on. "Don't let Earl take that away."

Brian barked a laugh and nodded. "You got it." He even gave him a mock salute.

David snorted as he shook his head. Striding through the restaurant, he glanced around for the sign indicating the direction to the restrooms. He spotted it on the other side of the restaurant and made his way across the floor.

As David entered the hallway leading to the men's room, he felt the hairs on the nape of his neck stand on end. He discreetly glanced over his shoulder as he pushed open the men's room door. While he didn't notice anything amiss—everyone appeared to either be focusing on their meal or their dining companions—the sensation persisted until the door was closed.

Having lived off his gut instinct for decades, David refused to dismiss the feeling out of hand. He made quick use of a urinal as he tried to decide how to play it. David figured whoever had been watching him could have just been admiring his fit body or looks. While he wasn't vain, he knew he was a pretty good-looking guy.

Except, that doesn't normally raise the hackles on the back of my neck.

After washing his hands, David used the towel to touch the handle and open the door. He set his foot against the door, keeping it open as he threw the damp towel in the trash. At the same time, David used the few seconds to peer around the bit of the room he could from his vantage point just inside the hallway.

Movement to David's right caught his attention—a man turning his head to gaze out the window.

David strolled forward, releasing the door. Using his peripheral vision as he moved back through the restaurant—keeping a row of tables between himself and the person in the booth to avoid suspicion—he took in the guy's profile. The man had on a ballcap and sat alone. He appeared more interested in whatever was outside the window than the partially eaten burger on his plate.

Just as David was about to lose sight of the man, the guy turned his head and looked directly at David.

David nearly missed a step as recognition hit him — Ulrick Lanston.

Shit. What is he doing here?

Just that fast, David knew the answer.

Nothing good.

Keeping his attention forward, feigning ignorance of the fact that a military black ops soldier who he hadn't seen in nearly three years sat on the other side of the same restaurant where he was on a date, David returned to his table.

David saw that dessert had arrived, and Brian had already dug in. His mate was chewing a bite, a blissful smile on his face. Before he'd even finished swallowing, Brian was already sinking the tines of his fork into the deep brown cone-shaped cake topped with hot fudge, ice cream, and whipped cream.

In truth, the dessert looked delicious. Eating it as he kept an eye on Ulrick would be no hardship. He glanced toward Lyle, but he knew he couldn't approach the man without tipping his hand.

Instead, David wondered if Brian had the man's phone number.

"You look like you're enjoying that, Brian," David commented as he settled back in his chair. He reached for a fork, ready to try some himself.

While David wasn't certain how, Brian must have picked up on his unease. Perhaps it was something in his training. He had been a marine, after all.

"Oh, yeah. You'll like this. It's delicious," Brian told him. Using his forkful of food to hide his lips, Brian asked, "What's wrong," before shoving the food into his mouth and humming appreciatively.

"Can't wait to try it," David responded, reaching out and sinking his fork into the decadent-looking dessert. The move hid most of his face from Ulrick's view, and he took advantage to say, "The guy in the ballcap sitting alone in the booth, other side of the restaurant kitty-corner to us."

David couldn't help but notice that the position gave the guy a good view of their table, and he had to fight back a blush as he tried to remember if he'd done anything that screamed *on a date*.

Shit. I shouldn't be thinking like that. No way should I be thinking about ways to hide my relationship with my mate.

"Got him," Brian muttered with a smile before eating another bite of dessert.

Before sliding his own forkful of food into his mouth, using the dessert to hide his lips, David stated, "His name is Ulrick Lanston. He was a sergeant first class in special forces last time I saw him nearly three years ago."

"Hmmm." Brian made the hum of interest sound as if he were appreciating his food.

As David chewed, he couldn't suppress a true smile and soft grunt. The cake was rich enough, but add in the fudge, and it gave his taste buds a sugar buzz. He worried adding some ice cream and whipped topping to a bite would send him into overload.

David swallowed. "Wow." Shaking his head, he used his fork to point at the dessert. "Just wow."

"Right?" Brian lifted his phone. "Need a picture."

Brian tapped on the device. As he placed it on the table, David noticed Lyle pull out his own. The detective's dark brow arched for a second before he smiled at Todd and showed him the phone. Todd smiled and nodded back before picking up his own phone.

"And the news is out," Brian stated with a grin and a wink. "The pack will know everything about Ulrick Lanston and what he's doing in Stone Ridge before the night is through."

Unable to help himself, David parted his lips in surprise. "Just like that?"

Brian nodded once, his smile still firmly affixed in place. "Just like that."

"Damn." David felt a measure of relief. Then it faded. Still keeping a smile on his face as he reached for another bite, he asked, "I wished I'd noticed him sooner. No telling what he overheard if he walked past us. I was too focused on our meals and you."

The corners of Brian's eyes tightened, betraying his mate's unease. The slight change to his scent did the same. There was a hint of pepper undercoating Brian's normally earthy, masculine goodness.

Good grief. Did I really just think that?

David's cat rumbled in his mind, telling him that the animal approved of the description, but it didn't care for their human being upset.

"I don't know how much more of this I can eat," Brian stated before shoving another bite into his mouth. As he chewed, he mumbled around his mouthful, "We'll deal with it."

Grinning, David nodded in response to Brian's comment even as he claimed, "Don't you worry. Just eat what you want." With a wink, he pulled the shrimp linguine bowl back toward him and claimed, "After I finish this, I'll finish that."

Brian's chuckle sounded warm and amused as he nodded, even though the lines around his eyes hadn't eased, yet.

Just as David finished the pasta, Earl appeared. "Hey, guys." He swept his gaze over the half-finished dessert. "Can I get you a box? Or anything else this evening?"

"No box," David assured. "I'll finish it."

A gleam of amusement entered Earl's eyes as he nodded. "All right then."

"Just the ticket, please," Brian instructed.

Earl nodded. "Be back with that in a jiffy."

After the wolf shifter had moved away, David leaned close to Brian and whispered, "Did he just say in a jiffy?"

"He did indeed," Brian confirmed as he set down his fork and relaxed back in his chair. With a half-shrug and a wry smile, he offered, "Country living at its finest?"

"Guess so."

They lapsed into silence as David tugged the dessert toward him and worked on polishing it off. He figured they could have taken it, but he didn't mind eating it. Besides, the ice cream would surely have melted by the time they returned to Markus's home.

What'll happen when we get there? Or . . .

"Where are we going after this?" David blurted out, shifting in his seat as his dick began to thicken anew. Even the uncertainty from Ulrick across the restaurant couldn't keep him soft. "I mean." David paused, feeling heat infuse his chest and rise up his neck, and he cleared his throat, fighting the sensation. "Uh, are we just heading back to Markus and Ronan's?"

Brian opened his mouth, then closed it again as his attention strayed to something over David's left shoulder. His mate pulled out his wallet. To David's surprise, he began thumbing through cash.

When Earl set the billfold with the ticket on the corner of the table, David understood.

"Cash is untraceable," Brian murmured as he glanced at the check. "And I had hoped to talk you into letting me take you back to my place for the night, but I didn't want to pressure you, either." After folding a number of bills and placing them in the billfold, Brian met his gaze once more. He moved his free hand to David's wrist and squeezed lightly. "But I think a call into Declan may be in order as we drive up the mountain. Don't you?"

David nodded, fighting back his disappointment. "I'm sure you're right." Then he stood, drawing away from Brian. He forced joviality into his tone. "Ready to head out?"

Brian chuckled as he stood and tucked his wallet away. "Definitely. If I eat another bite, you'll have to roll me out of here."

Despite the tension thrumming through David — caused by a couple of factors — he still laughed.

CHAPTER SEVEN

As soon as Brian started his pick-up, his phone rang. His older model didn't have a hands-free capability, so he handed the device to David. He wanted most of his attention on looking for a tail . . . just in case.

David quickly answered it and put it on speakerphone. "This is David with Brian. You're on speaker."

"Hello, David. Brian," a tenor voice greeted. "This is Prior. I heard you ended up spotting an old friend in the restaurant."

"Well, Ulrick was never a friend," David countered, his brows furrowing. "I can't even recall speaking to him, to be honest."

"Then how do you know it was him?" Prior asked, curiosity in his tone.

"I know him through his reputation," David revealed. "Even though nothing was substantiated, there were whispered tales of his wet work exploits."

"Hmmm," Prior mused, and the sound of typing could be heard through the line. "Interesting that news of a special forces asset's assassin work would leak."

"That is unusual," Brian commented, frowning. "Who the hell would reveal any hint of particulars regarding black ops missions?"

Prior grunted even as David just shrugged. "Whispers passed on in the dark. You know how it goes."

Brian wanted to know who started the whispers. Those

sorts of things could get a person in trouble damn fast. Spotting a vehicle in the rearview mirror, he glanced from it to the road and back again.

"We may have a tail," Brian commented.

"A navy pick-up?" Prior asked.

"Yeah," Brian confirmed.

"That'll be Beta Dixon," Prior told them. "He wanted to make certain you didn't end up with a tail, so he's going to be weaving behind you, criss-crossing on back roads." After a pause, he added, "Oh, and you're supposed to be going to the Rochette brothers' place. We're setting it up so it looks like you're going to a poker night after your dinner at the restaurant."

Brian didn't counter Prior since he knew he was the mate of the pack's head enforcer, Kajika—a dominant wolf shifter who appeared of Native American descent. Still, being surrounded by a bunch of others was the last way he wanted to end his first date with David. Unfortunately, Brian knew he wasn't going to get a choice in the matter. He understood the decision since there was no way he wanted to lead anyone to the secluded facility he was building.

"I don't know where that is," Brian admitted. He couldn't recall meeting anyone named Rochette. "Where are they?"

"I've just texted you their address," Prior told him. "Drive leisurely. It should take you about fifteen minutes to get there."

Then the line disconnected.

David made quick work of pulling up the information Prior had sent. Except, being so rural, there was no way a map app would work on his old phone.

Brian preferred the older flip phone because, with a couple of tweaks, no one would be able to use it to global position his ass.

"Uh, so, he sent a map, too." David sounded relieved. "We

just need to watch the road signs so we can figure out where we are and where we'll need to turn."

Chuckling, Brian muttered, "Well, that'll make it easy to take longer to get there."

David nodded as he stared out the windshield. He even leaned forward, perhaps watching for side roads.

After a couple of minutes of silence, Brian couldn't help but say, "This isn't how I'd hoped our date would end."

Glancing toward him before returning his attention to a street that they were passing, David muttered, "Looks like Pinedale Road." As he searched the map on the phone's screen, he added, "And this isn't the end of our date. This is just a detour. Oh, shit." David pointed behind them. "We were supposed to turn that way."

Scoffing, Brian slowed his pick-up as he searched for a place to turn around. He spotted a turnout and eased onto it. A few seconds later, a set of headlights appeared behind him so Brian waited. He watched Dixon's truck pass them before driving back onto the road, heading in the other direction.

Brian turned onto Pinedale Road. "Where do we turn next?" he asked, leaning closer to the wheel. "And what do you mean about our date?"

"We're looking for Ridgelyn Lane, and it'll be on the right," David told him before pinning him with a heated look. "And I mean, we're visiting a bunch of shifters for what looks like a poker game. We can do one of two things."

"One of two things?" Brian suddenly felt like a parrot, repeating the other man so often. He'd noticed himself doing it at the restaurant, too. He was just having such a hard time processing everything with the arousal emptying his big head of most thoughts. Clearing his throat, Brian asked, "What two things."

David seemed to hesitate for an instant. Then he reached over and placed his left hand on Brian's thigh.

Heat immediately rolled up Brian's leg, and his cock twitched. His mouth went dry, and he swallowed convulsively. His arms twitched, and he had to jerk the wheel to keep them on the road.

"Shit," David muttered, yanking his hand away. "Sorry."

Sucking in a harsh breath, Brian shook his head. "Please, don't apologize," he murmured hoarsely. "Liked it . . . a lot."

David stared at him for several seconds, as if trying to gauge if Brian was telling the truth.

Brian cast a heated smile in David's direction before returning his attention to the road. He had to concentrate damn hard to make out the road signs. His eyes weren't as young as they used to be.

Huh. Wonder if that'll change if I let David bond us.

Brian had overheard the things that could and would happen to a human after they'd been claimed by a shifter. A human's health and virility would increase, becoming less susceptible to colds and other ailments. Their senses, strength, and speed could heighten, although not to the point of a paranormal's. Even their bones would become stronger.

Plus, a human's aging would slow, and their life would be tied to the shifter's, who could live upward of five hundred years.

Considering David was a made shifter, not a born one, Brian wondered how that would correlate.

Will we live for almost five hundred years? Or will it be less?

David didn't think there was a person on the planet who could answer that question.

"My touch almost made you wreck the truck?"

Upon hearing the incredulity in David's voice, Brian scoffed. "Hell, yeah." He smirked at the man. "I'd still love to hear about those two options." Then Brian caught sight of a street out the window and slammed on the brakes. "Shit, sorry," Brian cried, reaching over to grip David's upper arm when he saw the man pitch forward into his safety belt. "This is our road."

"No problem," David replied, righting himself. A wry grin curved his lips as he stated, "Uh, the house we need is the third one on the left."

Brian breathed a sigh of relief as he nodded. He seriously needed to get off the road. The presence of the man next to him was beyond distracting.

Turning into the driveway, Brian followed the winding gravel path. The trees on either side gave way to a sprawling lodge-style home. It even sported an attached three-car garage as well as another shop-like building that could probably hold several more vehicles.

Four vehicles were already parked in front of the place.

David whistled in obvious appreciation, and Brian nodded in silent agreement.

"Sometimes, I wonder what these shifters do to be able to afford these homes," Brian murmured, knowing he would never ask. "They're paying for everything I'm doing, too."

"Wow." David just shook his head in clear wonderment.

Brian parked his pick-up beside another much newer model, then shut it off. After unbuckling his belt, he half-turned in his seat to face David more fully. To his pleasure, Brian watched David slowly mirror his moves.

Patience. My shifter doesn't seem to be as experienced or confident in his sexuality as I am.

With that mental reminder in place, Brian asked, "So, two things?"

David nodded, sweeping his gaze over Brian's face. "Right. Uh." Blowing out a breath, he seemed to be girding himself up for something. Then David's smile turned wry. "Why is it that saying these words seemed so much easier when you weren't staring at me?"

Brian hesitated, wondering how he could help David. Cracking a smile, he asked, "Would you like me to turn around?"

Scoffing, David shook his head.

To Brian's relief, the man smiled, too.

"No," David replied softly. "I don't want that." With a deep sigh, he reached out and took Brian's hand. For several seconds, he just stared at their joined hands. "You know," he finally commented. "I've never held hands with a guy before."

"I can't say it's something I've done much, either," Brian admitted. He squeezed David's hand, drawing his attention back to his face. "I like it, though."

David smiled. "Me, too." As he roved his gaze over Brian's face, his blue eyes heated. "I've never kissed a guy, either." Just that fast, he sobered as he admitted, "That desire was beat out of me when I was a teenager."

"I'm sorry that happened to you," Brian murmured, once again feeling the desire to hunt the asshole down. Unable to help himself, he asked, "Uh, is he, uh . . . still alive?"

With a shrug, David admitted, "I don't know." His eyes darkened. "And to be honest, I don't give a shit."

Brian wanted to question more, but he didn't know how to tactfully do it, so he decided to say, "I don't blame you."

To Brian's surprise, David shared, "I stopped talking to him midway through my second tour when he started asking me for money." His blond features darkened, and he growled, "When I was in high school, before . . . everything" — he winced but kept talking — "he told me he'd paid off the mortgage with my grandfather's life insurance policy after he'd died." David's jaw clenched, but before Brian could reassure him that he didn't have to share anything he didn't want to, the man stated, "My father didn't work. It's one of the reasons he figured out that I was . . . anyway. We didn't have a lot of money, he said. Just a monthly annuity payment from an accident payout that took my mother's life."

"Shit, David." *Fuck, the man sure had a shit childhood.* "I'm so sorry."

David shook his head and waved his free hand. "I didn't know her. Anyway, what I'm trying to say is, when dad started asking for money just after I started my second tour, I had a buddy look into his finances." His face clouded, and a muscle flexed in his jaw. "He'd mortgaged the house and was up to his eyeballs in debt . . . gambling debts. Guess without me there to beat on, he got bored and turned to other destructive activities." Shaking his head as his expression turned vacant, David murmured, "I told him no, and he tried to use a false identity to access my account. I was notified. I pressed charges." David shrugged as he stated in a cold tone, "Last I heard, he was doing fifteen for identity theft. That was six years ago. In the event of my death, everything I own goes to a foundation helping abused and battered youth."

Brian swallowed hard, trying to get his thoughts in order. Gently, he massaged David's hand as he tried to figure out something to say to that. Finally, he whispered, "You are one of the strongest men I know."

David snorted and shook his head. "No, I'm really not." Tapping his temple, he admitted, "I'm still plenty messed up, and I'm too afraid to do anything about it."

"Admitting you're messed up is the first step," Brian countered. "You'll take the next step when you're ready." Before David could say anything to counter him, Brian eased closer across the bench seat. "Now then. I really, *really* want to hear about those two things." Then he continued, "Or maybe I can guess."

When David went to open his mouth again, Brian pressed the pads of his forefingers over the man's lips. The hairs on his arms instantly stood on end, and heat hummed through him. He really wanted to replace his fingers with his own lips, but he didn't think that would be welcomed just yet.

Instead, Brian guessed, "We can go in that house, meet everyone, then play poker, as if that had been the plan for the evening all night." With a wink, he continued, "Or, we can go in there, meet everyone, then find a quiet nook and make out like horny teenagers."

David gripped Brian's wrist with his free hand and pulled his hand down even as he chuckled. "Make out like horny teenagers?"

Brian nodded.

Sobering, David leveled a serious look at him. "I've never done that before."

Shit. Had he fucked up already?

"I would like to, though." Releasing Brian's wrist, David reached out and touched his face, tracing along the edge of the beard that covered Brian's top lip. "Been wondering what this would feel like."

Sucking in a sharp gasp upon feeling the light, erotic touch, Brian found his attention straying to David's full lips. "I'd—" He paused and swallowed hard, trying to get moisture into his suddenly dry throat. "I'd be happy to show you."

David nodded slowly, sliding his hand from his lip to his jaw, the sensation of him feeling the facial hair there causing the hairs on Brian's neck to stand on end.

"For this first kiss," David whispered as he drew closer to Brian. "I don't want an audience."

"Anything you want," Brian replied, meaning it. As long as he got to feel David's lips against his own, he would agree to anything.

"Don't really want to make out in front of people," David continued to voice his thoughts even as his blue eyes darkened with his desire. "Don't think I'm that kind of guy."

"Good," Brian agreed. "Want you all to myself."

"Yeah. You, too."

Brian didn't get a chance to utter his pleasure because then

David pressed his lips to Brian's own. His touch was soft, tentative, as he slid his mouth one way, then another. He seemed to be exploring, seeing how they fit, and for a moment, Brian allowed him that.

Then . . . Brian's desire surged through him, and he needed more. While tightening his hold on the hand he still held, he lifted his other to David's head and gripped his nape. Brian used the hold to tilt his new and forever lover's head to the side as he nipped at David's bottom lip.

As soon as David opened, Brian took advantage. He thrust in his tongue, going deep, tasting the food and drink they'd enjoyed that evening as well as something else, something masculine and delicious and all David. Groaning his pleasure, Brian slotted their mouths together more fully and ravished the other man's lips and mouth.

For an instant, Brian realized that David had frozen, and he feared he'd pushed too hard.

A second later, David joined in the kiss, giving as good as he got, and Brian's senses sang from the sheer ecstasy given by a simple kiss.

CHAPTER EIGHT

For an instant, David had been shocked by the intensity of Brian's kiss. Never had someone taken his mouth in such a way. It fired his blood and caused his body to flush hotter than anything he'd ever before experienced.

Then David had felt Brian's lips hesitate against his own, and that had pulled him out of his momentary stupor.

David pushed into the kiss, sliding his tongue against Brian's, enjoying his rich flavor. Petting his jaw, he relished the feel of his soft facial hair under his fingers. Even the tickle of the shorter hairs against his lips created zings that traveled down his chest.

Kissing Brian felt like a full-body experience, and David knew he would never get enough of it. With the way his cock throbbed behind his fly, he eased even closer. He squeezed Brian's hand once, then released it in order to grip the man's upper arm. The idea of pushing Brian backward, so he could lever over the man pulsed through his sluggish brain. David could press against him, grind, giving him much-needed stimulation to his trapped dick.

He could—

The hard rap of knuckles on a window yanked David out of his lustful ideas. Shocked and a little embarrassed, he jerked backward out of Brian's hold. Gasping for breath, David peered around wildly.

For just a second, David felt certain he would see his father glaring in at him, his belt in hand, and fear surged through him, killing his boner faster than a bucket of ice water.

"Whoa, whoa, David," Brian crooned. "You're okay. It's okay."

David came back to himself with a snap, and he froze. Staring at Brian's hands, which were lifted in placation, he realized he must have been batting at him, as if to ward away blows. His breath came in ragged gasps, and he didn't know if he felt hot from the kiss or from the raging heat of embarrassment.

"You with me, David?" Brian asked softly.

"Yeah," David whispered, surprised at how rough his voice sounded.

Shit. Was I screaming?

Brian slowly reached for him, probably not for the first time. "Hey, you're okay," he crooned, resting his hands on his shoulders lightly at first. Then he slid them around him as he eased closer. "You're okay," Brian repeated, pulling David into a hug.

David froze for a heartbeat, then two, before sagging against the larger man. Burying his face against the crook of Brian's neck, he inhaled deeply. His mate's woodsy, masculine aroma sank into his senses, calming him faster than anything he could ever have imagined.

Even his cat purred in his mind as if trying to soothe him.

"I-I'm sorry," David mumbled against the fabric of Brian's shirt. "Can't believe I did that."

"Do you want to talk about it?" Brian asked softly.

David hesitated for a heartbeat, then two, before whispering, "Maybe later."

That was the best he could offer because, in truth, he didn't want to talk about it. Not ever. But after freaking out just because someone rapped on their truck window, he knew he really needed to get some help.

"Whatever and whenever you want," Brian replied quietly, gently rubbing a hand up and down his spine through his shirt. "I'm here for you."

Upon hearing that, David slowly lifted his head. He met Brian's dark-eyed gaze, those orbs full of warmth and understanding.

"Why are you being so nice about this?" David asked, needing to know. "You're not the shifter. Shouldn't you be running the other way from the broken shifter who doesn't know if he can ever give you what you want?"

"First off, you're not broken," Brian countered as he frowned, the move causing a crease to appear between his furrowed brows. "And I don't want to hear you say that. Maybe you're a little bent, but you're not broken." Before David could counter that, Brian added, "And I've seen and heard of enough shifter pairings to know that, when they both work at it, both people come out stronger for it. So, yeah, I'm not the shifter here, but I know if Fate paired you with me, then I know the work will be worth it." Brian's expression sobered as he pinned David with a solemn gaze. "But *only* if *both* work at it. Will you work at it with me, David?"

For just an instant, David thought he felt how a deer in the headlights felt. He could jump one way or the other. One way would take him to safety, and the other could very well mean his life. And just like a deer blinded by those headlights, David didn't know which way was the better option.

Then David's cat hissed in his mind, and he realized there really wasn't an option after all. The cat in his head would never walk away from this human. If David acted like an asshole and pushed Brian away now, all that would do was mean he would end up having to crawl back to the man and beg forgiveness. For Brian, David needed to be a better man.

Brian began to loosen his arms, easing his hold and drawing away from him.

David gripped Brian tighter to him, uncertain when he'd even wrapped his arms around the man. "Yes," he whispered sharply. "Yes, I will try." Grimacing, David added, "But please don't hate me when I fuck up. I've never been in a re-lationship before, with a guy or girl." When he saw Brian's lips loosen into the beginnings of a smile, David hurried to add, "And I know I'm fucked in the head. I'm totally aware of that. If . . . if"—he hesitated, uncertain he would be able to follow through, but needing to offer—"if you think I should see that psychiatrist guy, then I'll go."

Even if I sit there in silence every session, I'll still go.

Cradling the nape of David's neck, Brian told him, "If you want to go to the psychiatrist, then I'll support you, but an action like that, it's for you. Not me." He offered a supportive smile as he added, "And for the record, if you'd said no and wanted to walk away, I would have talked to your buddies and worked up some creative ways to change your mind."

"Really?" Surprise and an odd sense of pleasure flooded David in equal portions. "You would have?" When Brian just smirked, David had to ask, "How?"

Brian snorted as he shook his head. "Not sure, and I wouldn't tell even if I did know." With a wink, he began eas-ing his hold. "I will tell you, that between your friends' input and the frustration of that cat in your head, I bet it wouldn't even have taken that long."

"Wait," David cried, not bothering to try to counter the man, since he knew he was right. "Can we try that kiss again? Um, just so we can finish it properly?"

After Brian held his gaze for a few heartbeats, his bearded lips curved into a smile. "Of course."

Then Brian leaned back toward him.

That time, David met him halfway. Their lips touched, and it felt just as spectacular as it had the first time. He parted his lips and slid out his tongue, lapping at Brian's mobile append-age each time it darted away, and David moaned softly, real-izing the man was playing with him.

That knowledge only heightened the experience, as well as his enjoyment of the kiss, and David wanted more.

Except, when David tilted his head and tried to thrust deeper, Brian slowed the kiss, easing it to its natural conclusion, causing their lips to part with a soft pop.

While David didn't think they'd been kissing all that long, he was still out of breath, and he panted roughly.

Brian rested his forehead against David's, and he felt as if he were inhaling the man's spirit, or maybe his soul, with each breath they shared.

David finally managed to unscramble his brain cells a smidge, but he was still only able to whisper, "Wow."

A rusty chuckle filled the cab, coming from Brian. "Yeah," he agreed. "Wow." Then he lifted his head only to peck a quick kiss to David's mouth before he pulled backward. "And we should probably get inside. We've, uh" — he cleared his throat — "I think we've been out here a good twenty minutes."

David peered around and realized there were another three cars that hadn't been there when they'd pulled up. His cheeks heated for a whole new reason, and he groaned softly. "Oh, god."

Chuckling quietly, Brian squeezed his upper arm before releasing him entirely and reaching for the door's handle. "Relax, David. The guys here have seen some of the couples do plenty more than make out with each other."

"Damn, seriously?" David asked on a gasp even as he opened his own door. The cool air on his face and neck felt fantastic, helping him to calm down. He closed the door and rounded the vehicle to join Brian. "Please tell me they don't fuck in front of each other. I don't think I'd ever be ready for that."

Brian laughed and shook his head, much to David's relief. "Most definitely not," he assured. "Even though shifters are very demonstrative with their affections, kissing and groping and shit, they don't fuck in front of others." Then Brian winced and added the caveat, "At least, not on purpose. And if you ever happen to stumble upon a couple copulating, keep walking. They're actually extremely possessive and protective about who sees their mate in the throes of ecstasy."

"Good to know."

No way did David want to get his butt whooped by accident. While he hadn't seen any of that sort of behavior at Alpha Declan's lodge, he hadn't been certain if the average shifter get together was different. Even as David mentally cringed at the thought of seeing others fucking, he couldn't help but wonder what it would look and feel like to sink his hard dick into Brian's hole over and over.

What would his body feel like shivering with need against and around mine?

How does he look when his orgasm is racing through his system?

"Hi, guys," a deep voice greeted. "Sorry to startle you earlier." When David met the dark eyes of the goateed man before him, he recognized him as Kade, one of the pack's enforcers. "I only meant to tease."

Shit! Kade was privy to my meltdown?

Then it hit David, and he winced.

Not only had Kade been privy to it, but he'd also had a front-row seat because he'd caused it.

"I understand, Kade," Brian replied, not sounding upset in the least. "You didn't know that would bring back bad memories. We're good."

David just clenched his jaw. He didn't know what to say or do. These guys were all so open and understanding, when all he wanted to do was yell at the asshole for freaking him out. Except, David knew that wasn't fair because it hadn't been Kade's fault.

How was the shifter to know that a simple interruption of our kiss would send my brain flying into a tailspin?

Of course, he wouldn't.

Forcing himself to unclench his jaw, David jerked a nod as they climbed the steps toward the clearly worried enforcer.

He managed a tight smile he didn't feel. David even mentally shushed the annoyed grumblings his cat was aiming at the enforcer.

Kade grimaced as he reached over and opened the front door for them. "I really am sorry, man," he murmured softly. "I had no idea."

"For what it's worth," David began slowly, choosing his words carefully. "I didn't know I would respond like that either. I've never . . ." He glanced toward Brian before focusing on Kade again and admitting, "Brian's my first guy kiss."

Kade's lips curved into a wide grin. "Really?" He sounded so damn pleased for him. "Congratulations." Then he patted him on the back hard enough to make David rock forward a step as he winked. "Ya sure looked like ya were enjoying it." Then, to David's surprise, Kade's cheeks took on a pinkish hue as he muttered, "Until I fucked it up. I am sorry." Waggling his eyebrows, Kade teased, "You's was totally steamin' up the windows. Woo-woo-woo."

David chuckled at Kade's antics, unable to help himself. As Kade patted him on the shoulder, still grinning, and David followed Brian into the large home, he realized that was exactly what the wolf shifter had been trying to do. The man might be an enforcer, but he also knew how to lighten the mood.

Trying to keep the mood light, David asked, "So, uh, what do you do for a living, Kade?" He smirked. "Don't tell me stand-up comedy."

Kade chuckled. "Naw. I'm a mechanic." Cocking his head, he asked, "You find a ride, yet?"

David shook his head and admitted, "Haven't even looked, yet."

"What's your preference?" Kade asked as they moved deeper into the house. "Two wheels or four?"

"You guys ride motorcycles around here?" Brian questioned, looking surprised.

"Hell, yeah," Kade replied emphatically.

"Best way to get around these mountains," Nereo cut in, announcing his presence. With a grin that showed off his fangs, he added, "It helps when I have Warren clinging to my back, helping to keep me warm." The vampire who'd been instrumental in helping David recall . . . everything . . . turned his assessing dark-eyed gaze upon him. "How was your date, David?"

"Great," David replied. Even though he figured the vampire was asking about so much more, he continued, "The food at Caribou's is excellent." Then David lifted Brian's hand, which was in his own, although he didn't know when they'd done that, and brought Brian's hand to his lips as he peered at the older man. "And the company was even better."

Even as Nereo looked like he wanted to question David further, Warren appeared at his side and gave him a wink. "Glad to hear it." He looped his arm around the vampire's waist and told everyone, "Alpha Declan should be here any minute, so you should find a drink and make yourself comfortable in the rec room."

CHAPTER NINE

As it turned out, the rec room — or recreation room — was a massive space above the three-car garage. From the looks of things and the smell of fresh paint, Brian would guess that it had been finished fairly recently.

One-third of the huge area contained a number of sectional sofas clustered around a big-screen TV that hung on the wall. The section opposite contained a foosball table, dartboards, and several round tables that were set up for poker. A bar dominated the back wall, complete with a refrigerator and microwave. A pool table dominated the middle.

The place would have screamed man-cave if it weren't for the clearly domestic touches. There were colorful throw blankets over the back of several chairs, and vibrant pillows decorated the sofas. Doilies rested under each lamp that stood on end tables and floors. There were even small glass mosaic trivets to keep drinks off the wood.

"Wow." Brian watched as David picked up one trivet where the glass pieces were in the form of a really nicely done cardinal. He held it to the light, clearly admiring it. "This is impressive."

"Thanks, big guy." A slender man with shoulder-length, dark-brown hair sauntered around the sofa to stop beside them. "You would not believe how long it took me to find just the right shades of red for that thing."

David's jaw sagged open, and Brian had to agree.

"You made this?" David held out the item.

The guy nodded and took the piece. "Sure did." He placed

it back on the side table, then held out his hand. "Wendell Burgeon, although soon to be Rochette as soon as I convince the big lug to marry me."

Brian could see David's surprise in his eyes as he shook hands with the lithe, five-foot-ten-inch male and introduced himself. When Wendell shook Brian's hand, he felt the same. The guy's character more than made up for his size.

"So." Wendell rested his hands on his hips and glanced between them. "Which of you is the shifter?" Rolling his eyes even as he grinned, he admitted, "I'm human and can't always tell."

"I'm human," Brian quickly stated. Then he indicated David, who still seemed to be in a sort of state of shock. "David is one of the altered soldiers the pack rescued." With a shrug, he admitted, "We just met this afternoon and realized we were mates."

Clapping his hands together, Wendell bounced on his toes in obvious happiness. "Oh, guys! I'm so happy for you," he cried. Then he grabbed the cardinal coaster and held it out to David. "Please, take this. Consider it a congratulations and bonding gift."

"We, uh, we haven't . . . ya know," David stuttered softly even as he took the trivet he'd been admiring. "Um, done that yet."

"You will," Wendell replied, acting as if it were a done deal.

In truth, Brian figured it probably already was. After all, who in their right mind went against Fate?

Before either of them could come up with a viable answer, Alpha Declan walked into the room, put two fingers between his lips, and whistled thrilly.

Brian wasn't the only one who winced. Considering a paranormal's heightened hearing, it had to be so much worse for the others.

"Ah, got yer attention," Declan called happily. "Good. Everyone, have a seat, please."

As the alpha of the wolf pack moved toward a comfortable chair, everyone else scrambled to obey.

Brian did the same, gripping David's upper arm and leading him to a small sofa. As he settled beside David, he couldn't help but notice the way the man clutched the trivet to his chest with one hand. The grip he had on Brian with his other hand was incredibly tight. Unwilling to call attention to the near-painful hold, he rested his free hand on David's nape and massaged softly, helping him to relax.

By the time everyone had settled, David's hold had eased . . . then Declan opened his mouth, causing him to tense right back up again.

"It seems we have a situation," the alpha announced.

"Are you certain you want to come home with me?" Brian still couldn't believe that David had asked to return to his cabin with him instead of heading to the alpha's lodge with the rest of those on his team.

"Yes," David replied softly. His brows were furrowed, and his expression seemed troubled. "You keep asking that." Cocking his head, David touched his upper arm. "Do you not want me there?"

Shocked to hear the insecurity in David's voice, to see it on his face, Brian almost pulled the truck over to the side of the road. Only the urgency that they reach their destination kept his foot on the gas pedal. He did reach over and take David's hand, twining their figures together.

"I'm sorry my question made you feel that way," Brian stated. "I didn't mean to."

"You've asked that same question three times now," David pointed out.

Grimacing, Brian muttered, "Sorry. I didn't realize." Glancing the shifter's way, he admitted, "I guess I'm just surprised. I didn't think you wanted to bond this fast, and I know that once we get to my cabin, we're not going to be able to help ourselves."

"I, uh . . . what do you mean?"

Brian heard the confusion tinged with wary disbelief in David's tone. He didn't blame the man. While Brian had been interacting and learning shifter's habits for over a year, David had only recently awoken as an altered.

My poor mate still doesn't understand everything that's going on between us.

That's okay. I'll help him. I'll be by his side every step of the way.

With those thoughts in mind, Brian reminded David, "Remember our lunch together this afternoon? In my cabin?"

Good god. Was that just a few hours earlier? Time sure does fly when dealing with a shifter mating pull.

While Brian had seen it happen in both Ronan and Bailey, actually experiencing it was a whole different ball of wax.

"Uh, yeah." David drew the word out as if wary.

"Bailey pointed out that my cabin is saturated in my scent," Brian began slowly, hoping David would be able to draw the conclusion without too much help from him. "And he had to help you get your cat to leave."

When David groaned, Brian knew the man had guessed it.

"You think that if I walk into your cabin a second time," David guessed. "Then my cat won't let me leave until I've claimed you."

Brian winced. "Well, you kinda make it sound like a bad thing," he grumbled, squeezing David's hand to get his attention. "What are your reservations?"

It occurred to Brian that they'd never had the opportunity to talk about David's hang-ups because Brian really didn't have any. He would be proud to be the mate of a shifter, and everything he'd learned so far told him that David and he could grow into a fantastic couple.

"I'm worried that I'll be a shit lover," David muttered, rubbing the back of his neck with his free hand. "What if I can't please you?"

Biting back a laugh, Brian did his best to keep the amusement out of his voice. "Well, considering we both get boners any time we're near each other, plus the fact that kissing is explosive, I'm pretty sure all you'd have to do is touch me, and I'd blow." As much as it sort of sucked to admit that Brian became randier than a teenager any time he was near David, he hoped it helped to bolster the shifter's confidence a little.

"Um, what if I can't touch your, um, y-your dick?"

Brian clenched his teeth for a second due to the way David whispered the word dick as if it were something naughty.

God, I so want to murder his father. Hmmm . . . speaking of murdering. I happen to know a guy in the pack who used to be an assassin.

"Brian?" David sounded tense. "I-Is that a dealbreaker?"

Yanking his mind from his inappropriate thoughts, Brian glanced David's way and offered him a reassuring smile. "Look, I'll be honest. Do I want you to touch my dick? Hell, yeah." Brian would never lie to the man who would soon become his partner. "No, it's not a dealbreaker. There are many ways to pleasure a partner, and we'll find what works best for us."

Plus, Brian was banking on his cat shifter's curious nature to help David's human side in that area. It might take a few years, but he would bet his life that, someday, David would become comfortable fondling his prick.

Hell, after we bond, we'll have plenty of time.

"What if I can never let you near my ass?"

David's words were spoken so swiftly that they nearly slurred together, and it took Brian a moment to figure out what he'd said. By the time he did, David was attempting to pull his hand free, and his shoulders had slumped. He reminded Brian of a boy who'd had his puppy kicked . . . if he'd ever actually seen such a thing.

Fortunately, he hadn't.

Brian would have been in prison for murder.

Damn. I've turned into a blood-thirsty asshole over the years. Oh well.

Dismissing those random thoughts, Brian refocused on what he should be — David's misgivings.

"I guess we never did discuss our preferences in the sack," Brian mused, choosing his words carefully. "I'm a switch. Do you know what that means?"

"Uh, yeah," David replied, sounding uncomfortable. "You like both positions."

"Right." Brian glanced David's way when he felt the man squeeze and release his hand . . . as if trying to soothe himself that Brian was still there. After a quick squeeze back, Brian admitted, "It's been a long damn time since I've found sexual release with anyone, man or woman."

Just that fast, David's hand tightened on Brian's nearly to the point of pain. "You're mine," his shifter snarled, his voice lowering to a guttural growl. "No one else. Not ever."

Brian did his best to cover his wince, but he must not have succeeded.

"Shit!" David released Brian's hand, only to grip it in both his own and begin to massage his fingers ever-so-carefully. "I was afraid of this, too," he whined. "You're human, and I don't know my own strength sometimes. What if I hurt you? Like . . . really hurt you?"

David's voice sounded so injured that Brian's heart damn near bled for him.

Snagging one of David's massaging fingers, Brian squeezed tightly to get his attention. "We all make mistakes, but here's something to remember, okay?"

Brian watched out of the corner of his eyes, still keeping an eye on the road ahead . . . and the side and rearview mirrors. He knew that Beta Dixon was still supposed to be watching out for them—in a gray *Prius* now—but that didn't mean he shouldn't relax his vigilance. Brian's vigilance had kept him alive more times than he could count.

"You listening?" Brian persisted.

"Yeah," David murmured. "I'm listening."

"Okay, so you accidentally squeezed too tight, and it was a little uncomfortable." Seeing David's wince and chagrined expression, Brian quickly continued, "As soon as you realized it, you stopped." He squeezed David's finger again as he told him, "I know that you will never intentionally hurt me, and if something unexpected happens, I can tell you it hurts me, and you'll stop. I have faith in you."

"Why?" David sounded so damn confused.

Scoffing softly, Brian glanced David's way as he smiled at him. "Oh, David, because of how upset you are that you accidentally squeezed my hand too tightly. Hurting me hurt you, just in a different way." Then Brian smirked and added, "Besides, after we bond, I'll become tougher and faster, with stronger bones and immune system, so it'll be damn tough for you to squeeze my hand too hard again."

"Wait, what?" David looked at him in shock, his eyes widening. "Really?"

"Uh, did no one explain what happens to the human when they bond with a paranormal?"

David's brows furrowed, and for all the world, he appeared to be searching his memories. He opened and closed his mouth a couple of times, even as he narrowed and relaxed his eyes, too.

Brian would never tell David, but he thought the way the guy silently processed was damn cute.

"Uh," David finally murmured. "I guess if I was part of that conversation, I don't remember or didn't retain it."

Frowning, he muttered, "Or maybe I was too distracted waiting to hear my next order."

Grimacing, Brian nodded. He recalled being told about the horrible mind-altering that had been enacted upon Bailey's team. Not only had their memories been wiped by the government's military experiments, but they had been forced to serve a specific person without question.

Brian sure hoped no other teams were out there living the hell Bailey's team had been in—doing exactly what some asshole scientist told them to do as the man's bodyguards—until Bailey had showed up and freed them—sort of.

"Well, uh, here's what I know."

Then Brian explained what he'd overheard as well as been told by Markus, Ronan, and a few of the other wolves. The more he spoke, the more he was pleased by the loosening of tension in David's shoulders. The man nodded occasionally and asked a question or two, seeming to accept and process what Brian was telling him.

When Brian got around to the age thing, David sucked in a harsh breath. "I-I'm sorry." He swallowed hard enough to cause his Adam's apple to bob, easily seen even in the moonlight. "Are you saying that I . . . uh, we could live to almost five hundred years old?"

"Uh, well, not sure," Brian admitted. Seeing the confused crease of David's eyebrows, he told him, "A born shifter can live upward of five hundred years old. I don't think anyone knows if you'll live that long or if it'll only be a hundred years or a couple of hundred years."

"Still," David whispered, his voice filling with obvious awe. "A guaranteed hundred years." Shaking his head, he muttered, "Do you know how many people would kill for that?" David scoffed and added, "Even for the possibility at two hundred years?"

Brian sighed deeply, sadness filling him. "And now you

know one of the reasons why the military is capturing and experimenting on shifters."

David hissed under his breath. "Shit."

Exactly.

Then Brian turned onto the narrow dirt road that would eventually take him to his cabin. "Grab the *oh shit* handle, David, and hold on tight," he ordered as he slowed and planted his left foot on the floorboard for better purchase. "You're going to need it."

Once David obeyed, Brian slowly bounced them down the track that could barely be labeled a road.

Chapter Ten

W hen Brian had ordered David to hang on tight, he hadn't just been whistling Dixie. The road, if one could call it that, was rutted, overgrown, and full of potholes in inopportune places.

"Gee-zus," David cried when they bounced over a particularly vicious series of rocky bumps. "How the hell are people supposed to get back to you in a hurry with a road like this?"

Scoffing, Brian replied through gritted teeth as he wrenched the wheel to the left, narrowly avoiding a boulder, "In their wolf forms, of course."

David winced as his shoulder tugged uncomfortably. "What about those with pups who can't shift, yet?"

Just then, to David's heartfelt relief, a familiar-looking cabin appeared between the woods. He focused on his breathing as Brian drove around the left side of the structure. To his surprise, when Brian pressed a button attached to the sun visor that looked a lot like a garage door clicker, some kind of electronic optical illusion disappeared, revealing a small garage tucked between trees.

Brian drove into the structure before hitting the button again. A soft hum filled the air as well as a low grating sound, telling David that doors or something similar were fitting into place. The light around them dimmed and went out before suddenly illuminating a workshop-garage combo space.

"Wow," David muttered, peering around at all the half-assembled electronics. He wasn't a wiz by any means, but he'd been in the military long enough to recognize motion sensors, cameras, and infrared scanners. In a hushed voice, David asked, "Alpha Declan supplies all this to you?"

"He does," Brian confirmed. Instead of getting out, he turned and pinned a confused look on David. "What did you mean about pups who can't shift? Aren't shifters born . . . shifting?"

David snapped his attention to Brian even as he shook his head. "No. They start shifting around puberty, give or take a few years depending on the cub."

"Fuck me," Brian grumbled as he grabbed the door handle and shoved out of his truck.

"Yes, please," David couldn't help but quip. Even his blood surged south. It wasn't like he could stop it, regardless of the fact that a black ops soldier was lurking in the area for reasons that could only be nefarious.

Scoffing, Brian smirked at him as he hustled toward a side door. "Soon, Casanova," he teased. Pausing at the door, he pressed a couple of buttons on a panel to the left of it. A second later, the words *no large life forms in the area* flashed on the screen, and Brian focused on David. "When we get to the cabin, I know your need is going to start taking over. Please, give me time to call Alpha Declan first." Brian grimaced as he admitted, "The ability of cubs to shift and my shitty road was never something we discussed. I need to talk to the alpha about it."

David nodded, vowing to give Brian as much time as he needed. After all, his human was being more than patient and understanding with him. It was the least he could do to return the favor.

As soon as they made it into Brian's one-room cabin, David understood exactly what had concerned the man. His mate's scent permeated the space, sending the arousal in his body into overdrive. His cock throbbed, and his nipples beaded. His teeth ached, and he couldn't help but stare at the pulse point in Brian's neck.

Licking his lips, David wondered what Brian's life-giving fluid would taste like. He'd stuck his finger in his mouth after getting a wound or papercut many times over his life. What human hadn't? David figured Brian tasted so much better than the slightly bitter, salty iron of his own blood.

As David watched Brian head toward the living room, turning on oil lamps as he went, he grabbed the back of a dining room chair to keep from following. His attention focused on his mate's jeans-clad ass. He could just imagine the muscular round globes hidden under there, and he wanted to peel them apart so damn badly.

"David, I need you to focus," Brian growled, his voice deep, commanding, calling to the cat within him. When David snapped his attention to Brian's face, he saw the man's narrowed eyes and firm features. "I need to make a phone call. Remember, David?"

"Phone call," David parroted, trying to focus around the delicious aromas teasing his senses. "Right." Shaking his head slowly, David tried to get his mind to engage, but it was difficult. "I-I . . . holy shit," he muttered. "How did you know?"

David gripped the back of the chair tighter, hearing the wood creak beneath his grip, but he dared not release it.

"I've seen it happen to others, David," Brian told him softly. "That's why I thought our date away from here was so important." He held up his phone even as he slowly eased around the far side of the table, as if that was any barrier to David and his cat. "I wanted us to connect through something other than sex." Then he pointed toward the fireplace. "Can you make a fire? We're going to need it to stay warm this evening, and the task will give you something to focus on other than my scent."

Nodding once, David saw the wisdom in that. "Okay," he responded slowly. "Where is your kindling?"

Brian pointed toward the fireplace. "All the kindling you'll need is in the basket to the left of the hearth. The logs in the grate are dry and ready to be set. There are a half dozen more to the right of the fireplace." Then he indicated the back door. "You'll need to refill the basket beside it because I didn't have a chance to do that this afternoon. I'm sure you can find the woodshed."

David blew out a breath as he nodded slowly. Even as he understood the need for a fire, he also realized that this was a way to distract him. As far as David was concerned, that was okay. He knew he needed something to focus on in order to resist the desire to jump Brian's bones. Especially since, as ramped up as David was, he wasn't entirely certain he would have the ability to prep the guy.

Gods, I never want to hurt the man.

Plus, David couldn't remember a time he'd ever had to prep a guy in his life. He'd watched a few online videos before . . . before . . . just before. Any time he'd picked up a guy at the bar, however, David had expected him to take care of himself.

David knew he'd been a shit lover, even to women. Wanting to be better, he focused on the task Brian had assigned him. As he built a teepee from the kindling supplies, then started it on fire, David heard Brian talking with Declan in low tones, but he didn't attempt to listen in. He knew that Brian wasn't trying to keep anything from him. Instead, the man was trying to leave him alone so he could focus.

I appreciate that.

Focusing on his task, David had the fire roaring in no time. He kept an eye on it as he placed a couple of logs close to the hearth, ready to be placed on it. Then he headed outside to grab more so he could refill the metal crate.

The fresh air helped clear his senses, and he inhaled deeply, drawing deep, cleansing breath after breath in and out of his lungs. He knew it wouldn't last for long, but he took advantage of the few quiet minutes to center himself. With an armful of wood, he headed back inside.

David dipped his head, doing his best to focus on the scent being given off by the freshly split wood in his arms. His focus was so absolute that he didn't realize that Brian had moved until he rounded the kitchen counter. Then it was all he could do to keep from dropping the logs there in the dining room and pouncing on his mate . . . his naked mate.

Brian had already made up the sofa into a fold-out bed. Blankets and pillows were tossed upon it somewhat haphazardly, attesting to the fact that the man had hurried. Sprawling on the bedding, Brian lay on his side, and his head lay on the palm of one hand. His other arm was behind him, and it moved rhythmically, drawing David's attention.

David's nostrils flared as he caught the scent of Brian's arousal perfuming the air.

"Place the wood in the metal basket," Brian ordered, his voice coming out harsh and guttural. "Then wash your hands and get undressed."

Even as David's cheetah demanded they pounce on their mate, Brian's clear, direct orders helped him keep his beast in check. As he mentally shushed his animal and did as his soon-to-be lover had ordered, he reminded his cheetah that they would have their mate soon. The man was prepping for him, and he was their mate, and they had to make it good for him, to give him pleasure and bliss and ecstasy.

David felt his cheetah chuff in his mind, acknowledging that fact.

After filling the metal wood holder, David headed into the kitchen. The move brought him so very close to Brian, and he nearly lost his resolve. Only the steely glint of his mate's eyes and the man's hard expression kept him moving.

Once David had swiftly washed his hands, he made short work of his clothes. He started to toss them on the floor, but the order of, "Fold them and place them on a chair," stayed that instinct. Once more, David followed the other man's command.

"Now, then," Brian growled, lifting onto an elbow to eye him. He held up something as he stated, "Come to the side of the bed and stand at parade rest."

David slowly did as ordered, praying to whatever god cared to listen for control and restraint. When he reached the side of the sofa bed, he planted his feet hip-distance apart. After clenching and releasing his palms a couple of times, realizing they trembled, David finally managed to bring them behind his back, clasping one wrist with the other.

"Good, my mate," Brian murmured huskily, sweeping his gaze over David in obvious appreciation. "Let's get your pretty cock lubed up so you can take my ass."

Brian immediately put deed to word. He revealed he held lube, and after squirting a liberal amount onto already glistening fingers, he wrapped them around David's erection. Then, ever-so-slowly, Brian stroked him, greasing up his stalk in mind-numbing movements.

The first touch of Brian's hand on his cock nearly had David spurting. He rocked up, chasing his human's touch, going up onto his toes as he thrust. He dug his nails into his wrist because his mate hadn't given him permission to release the pose.

To David's relief, Brian eased his hand back down to the base of his shaft and stroked him all over again. His easy movements created a delicious heat that swiftly traveled through David's veins. His eyes grew heavy-lidded as he stared slack-jawed at where Brian pleasured him.

"That's the way, David," Brian crooned gruffly. "Just relax and enjoy. You'll get what you need as soon as I'm done fondling you."

David mewled—fucking mewled—but he couldn't have

moved away if he'd tried. The sweet ecstasy created by Brian's tight calloused fist was sending fire bursts up his spine. His balls were even beginning to roll in his sack, and his back began to arch as he punched his dick through the tunnel of Brian's fist over and over again.

"You're glorious in your pursuit of your pleasure, David," Brian rumbled huskily. "Are you ready to feel my ass instead of my hand? Want to fuck me, my mate?"

Even as David whined his need, he heard his cat snarl with demanding anticipation in his mind. "Yessss," he hissed. Still, he continued to rock, going onto his toes each time. "Pleeee-assse."

"I'm going to release your cock, David," Brian warned. "Then I'll roll over." His eyes narrowed as he pinned him with a feral gaze. "I expect you to enter me slowly. No matter how much you want to do otherwise, you'll do right by me . . . won't you?"

Gasping harshly, David struggled to string two words together, let alone a coherent thought. Finally, he managed to mumble, "Yes, sir."

"Good, David." Brian kept his dark-eyed gaze holding David's own as he slowly peeled his fingers from David's prick, creating a wash of needy tingles to erupt through his groin. "See that you do."

Then . . . Brian rolled over and stuck his ass in the air.

Yowling with need, David pounced. He grabbed Brian's hips and tugged them higher before palming the gorgeous globes on display before him. No one—man or woman—had ever showcased such muscled perfection, and David couldn't wait to sink his aching length between them.

David levered over Brian, gripping his base to guide his head to his human's stretched hole. Just the touch of his mate's muscled opening against his crown caused a cascade of zinging tendrils to wash through him, and he moaned. He felt his gums ache, so he opened his mouth, and his canines lengthened.

Need driving him, David began to thrust. His cock head slipped within the heated confines of Brian's body, and his eyes nearly rolled back in bliss. He tensed his hips, preparing to thrust, to sink deeply, to take what was his.

"David," Brian barked, his voice sounding strained. "You promised to take care of me."

A shudder went through David for a whole new reason, and compassion flared within him. His need to care for his mate exploded to life, burning within him like a wildfire. David moaned softly as he began mouthing sucking kisses up Brian's neck, murmuring platitudes the entire way.

"Ah, there you are, David," Brian crooned, arching against him. "That's the way. Like how you're easing into me. Keep doing that."

David hadn't even realized he'd been doing it, but when Brian said the words, he registered gripping, searing heat encasing over half his length. Moaning for a whole new reason, he barely resisted stabbing his mate so he could get the rest of his shaft inside his lover. His body shook as he barely hung on and kept rocking, sinking deeper and deeper.

Finally, after what felt like an eternity, David realized he was fully seated inside Brian's body. The lube-slicked heat encased him, and he knew he'd never felt anything so exquisite. David let out a low, yowling-moan that would have reminded him of his cat if he'd had a brain cell spare enough to think about it.

"God, you feel good, David," Brian rumbled from beneath him. He arched his back and nuzzled his butt against David's groin, sending his nerve endings into a frenzy. "Fuck me."

Unable to deny his mate anything—especially that demand—David obeyed. He pulled his hips back, withdrawing from Brian's exquisite heat, before thrusting forward again . . . and again . . . over and over.

Before David could even second-guess his move, he wrapped his teeth around the point of Brian's shoulder and bit.

CHAPTER ELEVEN

Rousing slowly, Brian couldn't remember the last time he'd felt so relaxed. He tried to recall what could have caused it. Then the arm around his waist tightened, and he felt a nose rub against his nape. Brian even heard snuffling.

Smiling, Brian recalled the night before—the highs and the lows.

One of the best highs of Brian's life was the three-orgasm-inducing claiming David had laid on him. At his age, he used to just appreciate getting a hard-on. With David, that never seemed to be a problem. For the man to fuck him into the comforter, sink his teeth into him, then fuck him into the mattress again—all three things causing orgasms of epic proportions, Brian figured he would become a bottom boy soon enough.

Of course, Brian knew that David still struggled with his demons. He couldn't imagine what had been going through his shifter's head for him to freak out in the truck from just a knock on the window. Brian was even too worried to ask.

Maybe he'll be ready to share someday.

Another thing he appreciated was the fact that David listened with earnest when Brian explained things. He wasn't dismissive or short. Instead, he seemed to honestly try to understand from Brian's point of view—as could be seen from how he took to Brian's explanation of his gramps' advice about respect, trust, and dating.

Of course, Brian also couldn't forget the fact that Sergeant First Class Ulrick Lanston was lurking about. According to Alpha Declan's people's research, the guy was probably in the area to carry out a black op. They couldn't find any actual orders that would put the man in their vicinity, which was definitely a bad sign.

The pack was gearing up for an attack.

That reminded Brian of his call to Declan the evening before. He couldn't believe — and evidently, the alpha had been just as chagrined — that they hadn't given any consideration to the state of Brian's road in conjunction with fleeing pack with young. As it was far too late, considering Ulrick's presence, the alpha was putting together alternate means of transportation to their sanctuary.

"You're thinking way too hard for first thing in the morning," David muttered, cuddling closer. His tone even turned petulant as he whined, "Why? What's wrong?"

Deciding he'd done enough thinking for the moment, Brian carefully turned so he faced his lover. "Nothing wrong." When David welcomed him into a long tongue-dueling good morning kiss, he hummed appreciatively. Brian broke away when breathing became paramount, murmuring huskily, "Everything is just right."

Then Brian grabbed the lube, which caused David to perk right up — his attention, not his dick. His dick was already hard against Brian's thigh. With a studious shifter watching and helping, Brian taught David how to stretch him before he welcomed his shifter's morning wood deep within his body.

After a hearty breakfast of bacon and eggs, Brian began walking David through his morning chores. One of those chores was indeed collecting said eggs.

"Holy shit," David muttered, staring at the apparatus stretching between the trunks of the trees. "How the hell did you create this?" Shaking his head, he added, "*Why* did you create this?"

Brian crossed his arms over his chest and stared up at his

invention. "Well, I admit, it wouldn't work in most normal forests, but here, where wolf shifters constantly patrol and keep wild cougar and lynx away"—he continued to grin as he shrugged—"a treetop chicken coop works just fine." With a wink, Brian beckoned before starting toward a hidden ladder. "Besides, most people don't look up, so they're safe up here, and they won't give away our location." As Brian stepped into a large pile of bird poop, he winced. "Much."

He still hadn't completely worked out the kinks. For example, how could he hide all the chicken excrement that ended up on the ground?

David continued to stare in wonder even as he followed Brian.

Brian showed off the hidden switch that lowered the concealed ladder. Then he revealed the opening in the wire-enforced mesh that surround the nearly five acres of treetop walkways. Most of the stretches were only usable by the flock of three dozen chickens Brian kept, but there were enough wooden bridges for him to get to the coop and back, plus most places that the chickens frequented. It had taken Brian a while, but with careful study, he'd figured out where the chickens enjoyed perching the most, and where they might hide eggs outside the hen house he'd built for them. With the entire structure consisting of five acres, the birds would always have more than enough bugs to eat, so Brian never had to feed them.

After they'd collected several dozen eggs, Brian led the way back to the opening, then the ground. As expected, he found Chasis, in wolf form, waiting at the bottom. Brian had been told the blond wolf youngster was actually a teenager and a tracker in training, but he'd never seen him in human form. Brian just knew him as a gangly, slobbery, happy-go-lucky wolf.

When Chasis yipped in greeting before swiping his tongue

over Brian's forearm, David snarled, curling his lip and revealing a canine. Chasis skittered back a few steps, tucking his tail between his rear legs. He hunched his shoulders as his canine visage glanced from Brian to David and back again.

"Damn it, David." Brian smacked the back of his hand against David's chest. "Stop freaking out my help."

"He licked you," David growled between clenched teeth, which only caused Chasis to whimper and skitter backward a few more steps.

"Of course, he licked me." Brian did his best not to roll his eyes when David continued to scowl at him. Lifting his hands, he set the big basket of eggs on the ground. "Okay. Let's get introductions over with." Placing one hand on his hip, Brian pointed at David. "David, I would like you to meet Chasis. He's a young wolf shifter who comes every morning and takes my eggs to our pack." Turning, he indicated a still cowering Chasis. "Say hello to Chasis, David."

David growled softly under his breath for an instant. Except, that just caused the wolf to whine again, his confusion clear. To Brian's relief, even David had the decency to groan and flush.

"Shit, pup," David muttered. "I'm sorry for freakin' ya out." Rubbing a palm over his mostly-short scalp, he continued, "Brian is my mate, and you slobbered on him. I know ya was just bein' friendly, but we just met, and me and my cat . . . we're still getting acclimated, so . . . could ya not do that again for a while? Huh?"

To Brian's surprise, the more David rambled, the more relaxed Chasis became. By the time his cheetah had stopped his verbal diarrhea, Chasis was sitting up straight and his tail wagged about a mile a minute. Even his butt end nearly vibrated with the activity.

Chasis yipped several times and began dancing around them. He bumped his nose against David a couple of times, before the man realized the young wolf was looking for pets. After a couple of ear scratches, Chasis barked again and went to Brian's side, bumping him instead of licking.

Brian chuckled and gave the youngster a couple of ear rubs. Just that fast, Chasis pulled away and trotted over to the huge basket of eggs. Laughing, Brian picked up said basket and started toward the cabin, both Chasis and David following.

As expected, in the middle of his small back porch, Brian found a cloth bag full of empty egg cartons. He quickly filled each carton, even having a half dozen leftover, and asking David to get his nearly empty carton from the fridge. As his cheetah did that, Brian carefully placed five dozen eggs into the cloth bag, then positioned the handles up and held them out.

Chasis yipped once more, then carefully wrapped his teeth around the handles. With care, he trotted off the back deck and disappeared into the forest.

"Okay." David knelt beside Brian, holding out the carton. "I'm so confused."

Brian smirked at his shifter. "You really think I can eat six dozen eggs a day?" With a roll of his eyes, he placed the extra eggs into his carton, then picked up the dozen he'd kept for himself. His thigh trembled a little as he rose, and David wrapped a hand around his waist to help him. Instead of commenting on it, Brian simply said, "Thanks. Anyway. Chasis comes every morning with a bunch of cartons. I fill them, and he takes them back to his ma. She distributes them to the pack." With a shrug, Brian admitted, "I have no clue who gets what, but Declan put her in charge of it, so I know the eggs won't go to waste."

David nodded slowly. "Okay. I get it." He peered back toward the hidden sky-high hen coop. "Um, I'm almost afraid to ask where you have the goats."

Brian laughed, recalling telling at some point during their

meal that he kept a herd of a dozen goats. "I'll show you. They don't need feeding right now, but it'd be good for you to familiarize yourself with them anyway."

Except, Brian didn't make it there. The small wristband he put on every morning vibrated, catching his attention. Growling softly, Brian uncurled his cuff to check the color.

Orange.

"Shit," Brian muttered, drawing out the word. "Come with me."

To Brian's relief, David didn't say anything. He just followed. He picked up the eggs and strode into his cabin, keeping a smile on his face and pretending nothing was amiss. After placing the eggs in his fridge, Brian moved to his laundry room.

"Since you're moving in here," Brian began without preamble. "I'm sure you'll want to know how to use the washer and dryer." He began thumping lids as if he were loading it. "Just remember to go easy on the detergent," Brian warned inanely as he pushed a wooden crate to the side, revealing a trap door. "If you don't, these smaller styles will end up overflowing with suds."

Fortunately, David caught on quickly. "Gotcha," he replied, although his expression appeared speculative as he eyed the hatch. "Halfsies on the detergent." Scoffing, David added, "I won't forget. I bet that's a fucking mess to clean up."

Appreciating his lover's adlibbing, Brian forced a chuckle. "Oh, that it is. I don't recommend it." Then Brian started the washing machine on a small empty load, just for the noise factor . . . and just in case anyone was actually listening.

Finally, Brian lifted a finger to his lips in the universal *hush* sign and led the way down the ladder and into his underground tunnels.

Once David was down, Brian hurried back up. He gripped a string that was attached to the wooden basket, so when he closed the hatch, the crate would slide back into place on top of it. Not only that, but Brian always had a towel set on a hook that would tilt with the pull of the string, dropping the towel to the floor, hiding any possible slide marks. Finally, Brian threw a lever that would lock the crate in place, not allowing anyone to follow them without considerable brute force—or ordinance—even if they did find the entrance.

Brian quickly returned to the bottom of the stairs. When David opened his mouth, obviously intending to question him, he held a finger to his lips again. Once David dipped his chin in a nod, Brian hurried through the tunnels.

Hearing David stumbling behind him, Brian suddenly realized that it was pitch black. He rolled his eyes at himself. Of course, shifter or not, the man wouldn't be able to see. Because Brian had made the space, he knew it like the back of his hand and could easily traverse it in the dark—David, not so much.

Brian took a few more steps, then felt along the left wall. He found what he wanted—an oil lamp. After pulling out a box of matches from that same nook, he struck one and carefully lit the lamp.

Peering left, Brian noticed David wincing and covering his eyes.

"Sorry about that," Brian apologized with a grimace. "I've been down here so much, I don't even bother with these most times anymore." Holding out the lantern, he stated, "We're almost to the control room. Then we can contact Prior and see why he alerted me. Shit, I hope Chasis is okay."

The young wolf hadn't been gone all that long, and Brian hoped he hadn't been caught in the crosshairs of . . . whatever was going on.

"Shifters have an excellent sense of smell," David murmured, rubbing Brian's back soothingly. "I'm sure he'll find a place to hole up and hide, if need be."

Brian sure hoped so as he nodded and led the way down the corridor and to the right. At a nondescript door, he pushed a code into the panel and it slid open. While Brian wasn't a computer genius by any stretch of the imagination, he knew how to take direction well. Show him something once, and he remembered.

Once David had followed him into the room, Brian quickly punched a code to close and lock it behind them. Then he crossed to the keyboard and the array of screens. Reaching under the desk, Brian felt for the discreet indent that would have his systems firing up. As Brian watched the screens flicker to life, never had he felt more relieved than knowing that he'd finished putting up the security system just the prior afternoon on the north end.

Still, it didn't surprise Brian at all when, once loaded, his systems showed a force creeping toward them from the east. He shook his head and rolled his eyes.

"Really?" Brian grumbled under his breath. "Rookies."

"What do you mean?" David glanced from the screens to Brian and back again, his concern clear. "What's going on?"

Brian took David's hand in his own and squeezed lightly. "It means, these assholes fell for the oldest trick in the book." Upon seeing David's brows furrow, he snickered. "Decoys."

CHAPTER TWELVE

Staring at the screens, David felt his brows shoot up. "Decoys," he whispered, understanding.

Each screen showed what looked like a computer mainframe hidden within a bunch of trees. There were booby traps surrounding each. David could tell by the outlines glowing on the screen — everything from pig snares to deadfalls.

Obviously, someone wanted a few prisoners alive to question.

That wasn't what interested David, though. "They're following the heat signatures," he mused, frowning as he watched nearly a dozen commandos creep toward each of the three false targets.

Brian nodded slowly. "Yep. Those have been up for nearly six months." Scoffing, he admitted, "I'd damn near forgotten about them with everything else I've been building."

"What do you mean?" David found himself fascinated as he watched trap after trap go off.

Some of the men screamed as they were lifted high into the air in a pig snare. Some didn't get a chance as spikes sprang from an embankment, skewering them, ending them instantly. Many of the men froze, peering left and right, up and down, as if trying to figure out where the next trap might lay.

David had to hand it to Brian . . . or whoever had come up with the traps. Even with them outlined on the screen, he was having a hell of a time figuring out any dimensions to them. He couldn't tell what kind of trap was what until it went off and something happened to the victim.

Ouch.

Seeing a spike stab a soldier through his eye socket, David grimaced and turned away from the screen. "Who built all these," he whispered, unable to contain his curiosity. "How?"

"Well, it was a concerted effort on the pack's part," Brian told him, not sounding at all concerned by what he was witnessing. "The inner circle tossed about a few ideas, adjusting some that were used for hunting." Waving his hand at the screen negligently, Brian told him, "I know what you're thinking. Probably something sad or sympathetic for these guys, but you need to think of it like war."

David knew exactly what Brian was talking about, and he did his best to compartmentalize his emotions. "Right," he muttered before grabbing a rolling stool and moving it beside Brian's. "So, what was that alert, and what do we do? Are any of our people in danger?"

Brian grinned at him. "Now there's the partner I need in this endeavor." Just as quickly, he grimaced. "Sadly, not much needs to be done on our part until it's clean-up time." Sighing deeply, Brian muttered, "That's always the easiest, messiest, and hardest, all at the same time."

"Uh, what?" Confusion flooded David.

Pointing at the screen, Brian explained, "This is the east woods. It's close to hiking trails. It's why we put those indicators there in the first place." Even as Brian curled his lip and his words came out a growl, he continued to explain. "We knew they'd come eventually, and we wanted to know what kind of numbers to expect." Brian shook his head. "Three dozen . . . and they're probably a small incursion to the assholes who want this pack. Now, we can shore up our defenses and really get ready."

"Ready for what?" David almost didn't want to know.

Brian's smile appeared grim. "War, David." With a shrug, he told him, "We're facing war."

David rubbed his palms over his face before he lifted his

attention back to Brian. "You can bring on the good news any time now."

Scoffing, Brian pointed at the screen again. "How about, in less than ten minutes, we took out three teams of commandos?"

Groaning, David shook his head. "That's not good news. There are three dozen more where they came from."

Brian winked before he rolled to the computer. "Yup, but they won't be coming here."

David watched as Brian began tapping a few quick strokes onto the keyboard. "What are you doing?"

"Activating a worm that Raul set up," Brian stated, continuing to tap at the keyboard, albeit more slowly. "Aaaaand . . . there it goes." He sing-songed his last few words as he stared at the screen.

Shaking his head, David muttered, "I have absolutely no idea what that just meant."

Grinning broadly, Brian turned to face him, his bearded lips creasing widely. "Truthfully? I'm not sure, either. I just trust these guys that it works." He shrugged, totally unconcerned.

"Aaaand, what's it supposed to do?" David couldn't help but ask.

"That worm is going to seek out every document and every file that says those three coordinates." Brian pointed at the still glowing tower-like stumps on the screens. "The worm will change each and every one of those coordinates to somewhere in a country we're not supposed to be in. If anyone goes looking for these teams, all they'll find is dead ends, false leads, and a whole lotta problems."

"Seein' as they're not supposed to be there in the first place," David whispered, finishing Brian's thought. "Damn."

Brian winked. "Exactly." Then he grimaced as he stared at the screens and shook his head. "However, in order for that to all happen, we gotta go do clean-up now." Brian waved at the monitors. "Get all these yahoos, alive and dead, outta here asap."

David rose to his feet. "Sure. I'll help in any way I can."

Almost twelve hours later, David regretted his offer. He'd been rounding up body parts, cleaning up intestines, and hiding blood trails for hours. He stank up to high heaven, and he hadn't seen his lover since they'd reached that stretch of mountains and been assigned to a clean-up crew.

"Hey, go get cleaned up," Kade encouraged, slapping him on the back. "Thanks so much for your help."

"Is Brian about finished?" David asked. No way was he leaving the mountain without his mate.

Kade nodded. "Yep. He caught a ride with the blue shuttle crew. He'll probably get home before you will."

"Not likely," David grumbled as he whipped his disgusting shirt from his body. "I'll race him there."

Laughing, Kade gave him a thumbs-up as he told him, "I'll gather these up and burn them for you."

David scoffed as he shucked his jeans. "Thanks." Then he started his shift.

Before long, David raced through the trees in cheetah form. He couldn't wait to see Brian. If he was lucky, he would indeed make it back to the cabin before the other man. That way, David would be able to wash the man from head to toe.

David had never showered with a lover, but he sure wanted to try it with Brian. A wet mate appealed to him in a way he didn't understand. In fact, even his cheetah wanted to discover what swimming with Brian would be like.

Go figure. Cheetahs enjoy water.

Reaching their cabin, David spotted the open back door and barely slowed. His need to catch his mate in the shower was too great.

It wasn't until David was in the middle of shifting that an odd scent caught his attention.

As David rose to his feet, ignoring his nudity, he searched the area . . . only to suck in a breath of shock.

Ulrick Lanston sat at the dining room table.

Somehow, David had raced right past him.

Raising his hands defensively, David growled softly. "What are you doing in my house, Ulrick?" he demanded, even though he could honestly guess.

Lifting his chin, Ulrick met David's gaze.

To David, Ulrick appeared to be searching for something, which confused the hell out of him.

An instant later, Ulrich blinked a few times as he cocked his head. "I don't remember much, but you're David Preston . . . aren't you?"

David slowly lowered his hands, ever mindful of the shower he could still hear beyond the curtain — *thank god Brian decided to close the curtain.* "Yes," he replied. He swept his gaze over Ulrick, searching for anywhere the man might be hiding a wire or bug, but David couldn't find it. "Why?" Then what Ulrick had first said stuck out. "What do you mean that you don't remember much?"

Ulrick rocked in his chair a little, blinking swiftly. He seemed to be having an internal debate with himself. Finally, he muttered, "I know my name, and that I'm military. I followed a general. Uh, General Sackett." Shaking his head, Ulrick muttered, "But I haven't been able to find him for weeks, and I don't have any orders." Ulrick rubbed his forehead as if he were in pain. "But your name came to me, so I found you." Lowering his hand, he pinned his cold gaze on him and stated, "There was an ops team infiltrating your territory, so I showed myself, so you'd be on alert." His smile turned a little creepy as he stated, "It worked. You're safe, so now . . . you can help me."

David wasn't entirely certain he wanted to know what the crazy man wanted, but he asked anyway.

"Help you how?"

Ulrick curled his lip and stated, "Help me remember who the fuck I am."

Well, shit. Now that Sackett is gone, just how many of his experiments are going to crawl out of the woodwork? And whose side will they end up on?

ABOUT THE AUTHOR

Charlie started writing fantasy when she was eight, and after stumbling onto her first erotic romance at age nineteen, she realized her true calling. She now focuses on writing gay erotic romance, normally of the paranormal variety, with heroes of all kinds. With the help and support of her husband, Charlie finally fulfilled one of her life-long goals . . . move to acreage with her horses. You can often find her curled up with her laptop and a cup of tea or glass of wine, creating her next adventure. Charlie enjoys exploring the mountains of her new Oregon home on horseback, 4-wheeler, or motorcycle.

She can be reached at ch.richards2010@yahoo.com

Or visit her at www.charlie-richards.com.